A Chill in the Air

A Collection of Stories and Poetry

A Chill in the Air: A Collection of Stories and Poetry

A Chill in the Air:

A Collection of Stories and Poetry

By

Storm Sandlin

Edited by

Mariah S. Ramer

Not suggested for readers under the age of 13.

First Edition

First Printing

ISBN-10: 1514795655

ISBN-13: 978-1514795651

Dedicated to the following lovely ladies:

Bernice E. Smith, whose love, imagination and creativity inspires us daily

Jewel A. Arnold, whose love, support and kind words have helped more than you know

Alma K. Williams, a loving, strong angel who watches over us

A Chill in the Air: A Collection of Stories and Poetry

Table of Contents

A Chill in the Air: A Collection of Stories and Poetry

Petrifying

Poetry

A Chill in the Air: A Collection of Stories and Poetry

The Threshold

An ominous house stands on a forgotten, cursed yard

Windows broken, shattered, and shard

Circling overhead, black ravens on guard

Awaiting inside, once a great beauty - now marred

No one has escaped this witch unscarred

She sees their fate with her tarot card

She knows you are coming, she cackles hard

If you dare cross her threshold black magic will bombard

Just a Game

Ruby flames of candles flicker and the night air is still

I watch the board as the eye moves to the spirits' will

The other side is coming through, I hear the moans

A portal is now open, the clock chimes echoing tones

Supernatural forces surround, this is nothing like I
planned

Deep fear overcomes me, I cannot move, frozen I stand

M-U-R-D-E-R the word is spelled, my heart races

On the wooden floor I hear disembodied paces

Sandlin

The flames burn out; I am not alone in the dark

A haunting song, words unknown sing like a devilish lark

I am blind in the shadows, looking for a way out, I seek hope

Ice cold hands hold me; this is beyond anything I can cope

Laughing of this demonic, unholy thing fills the room

My last breath exits my body, I know inescapable doom

I now look down to see myself just a lost soulless shell

It was just a game; I'm in a shadow filled world where nothing is well.

The Hidden Cavern

There is a cavern dark and deep

Where terrible things lurk and creep

The very few who are most brave

Travel into the depths of this awful cave

Brave they are but truly foolish

For waiting inside is something ghoulish

In the darkness there is a beast

Laying in wait for its next feast

Before you enter say goodbye

There is no escape, you will surely die

Those Who Live in the Shadows

Those who live in the shadows watch me walk down the hall

Those who live in the shadows my name they do call

Those who live in the shadows wait for me to fall

Those who live in the shadows are monstrous, not small

Those who live in the shadows know all

Whispers

Each night as I lay in my bed

My heart is weighed down with dread

My eyes close, eerie voices fill my head

The things they tell me should never be said

I wake in the morning, my hands covered in red

The Flock

The sky turns black as ravens eclipse the sun

Ebony flashes fly by, when will this be done?

A frenzy of them swoop down for feeding time

You wonder why this is, no reason, no rhyme

They land upon the unsuspecting crowd

Feasting until they have had their fill

Faces are hidden in this consuming black shroud

They have no emotion, no guilt as they kill

In the terrorized streets the people lie

Bloody and dying, most missing an eye

Why run? They will see you from the sky

A Haunting

There is an old brick house that sits on top of a hill

The stories that are told of it are terrible and real

It beckons you with its beauty, mystery, and thrill

Upon entering you are fascinated, filled with awe until

A gust of wind surrounds you in an overwhelming chill

You know that you are not alone, this spirit wishes you ill

A fierce shriek fills your ears, terrifyingly shrill

There it is now, coming for you, with eyes that long to kill

In your absence once again the house is completely still

The Disturbance

As I slumber in the dark peace of night

I'm awoke by the stinging blade of a knife

In the blackness I still have no sense of sight

I know this will be the end of my life

I'm grabbed and pulled down the stairway

Crying out for mercy, I make my pain aware

Struggling to no avail, I can't get away

This ruthless unknown killer goes on without care

I am drug through thick grass to a hole in the ground

Put in a wooden box, fastened shut with many nails

Covered in dirt, the weight muffles every sound

My attempts to escape are feeble and frail

As I lay in silence I wonder how I came to this terrible fate

What had I done to deserve such violence and hate?

The Hexed

A mirror knocked off from the dresser, ragged shards lay around

The shaker falls, millions of salt grains laying on the table abound

Black cats race in front of paths, causing misfortune where they roam

Inside silent homes umbrellas open, releasing a hex an unholy dome

Horseshoes on the blacksmith's wall flip upside-down 1, 2, 3 times in a row

Black ravens fly overhead; their shadows are cast on the grass by the dim sun's glow

Spirits full of malice follow where you lead, you have been cursed by the evil eye

You cannot break this circle of impending doom, no matter how hard you try

Mourning

In the funeral home, full of mourners, all these loved ones gathered in one place

Lining the walls hundreds of flowers fill many a vase

Unaware of whom I came to see, I walk slowly in disgrace

Looking into the satin-lined coffin, I see what no one should, my own face

Giggles

A small car with a team of painted faces

Comes to my house when I am all alone

They make their way in with their teeth filed sharp

Their mindless laughter echoes through the hall

Revealing knives hidden in their cotton candy hair

I fall to the floor in terror as they come over me

Yes it is I

Yes it is I, the one who sends chills down your spine

Yes it is I, the one who flashes behind you in the mirror

Yes it is I, the one who makes the untraceable sound

Yes it is I, the one who whispers things in your ear

Yes it is I, the one who stares holes into your soul

Yes it is I, the one who makes your nightmares come true

Creak

Alone
There are
Strange foot steps
Coming down my stairs
Creaking beneath each step
Slowly coming closer and closer
My heartbeat grows louder and faster
I have counted and there are no stairs left
They are down here, I know there is no escape

Glowing Eyes

Bright yellow eyes stare down at you

They are always watching, nothing you can do

Down the street from tree to tree it does follow

It hears you breathe, it hears you swallow

Through the dark you hear its haunting call

You run faster and faster and fear you will fall

The owl flies on, the last thing you see is its eyes' glow

Your body lies there, pecked by the crows

My Bed

As I laid in my bed

I heard haunting things being said

Strange voices full of dread

Like stories I have often read

These safe covers I dare not shed

Is my imagination just being fed?

Claws pull me though, leaving a pool of red

The Haunting of...

One night a ghost did appear

Like white silk transparent and sheer

Creating a frigid chill in the air

Filling my heart with dread and fear

I laid there frozen as it drew near

A scream filled my throat but I did not dare

This thing was after me, I was caught in its snare

Held prisoner by that empty stare

The being's pain and torture it could not bear

I came to nothing by this spirit's blinding white glare

Now I roam the earth alone, all mortals should take care

The bump in the night may be me, you have been warned, beware!

The Dining Hall

Many bones picked clean

Deep red blood stains gleam

Hear their meals scream

Eaten by a cannibal team

Achieving their evil scheme

The Seer

Crisscross threads seal my eyes and lips

I am silent and blind to all the world

Now my sight is of the mind and true

On paper I write with ink and wisdom

My last visions were of you and your fate

Tell the undertaker you'll see him soon.

Come Night

As Night falls and you begin to drift off into a dream

Darkness changes the world around you, nothing is the same

Shadows overlap each other as they move across the wall

What is real and what is imagination?

Sudden fears causes your heart to race

None of this is real you tell yourself, why don't you believe it?

The air turns thick and breathing is hard

Doom seems to beckon, your name is whispered about

The shadows are coming closer; there is no way to avoid your fate

Movement is impossible, you try to no avail

The night is now over and the shadows are gone

One trace is found, an unmade bed sets empty

R. I. P.

Many black roses lay on my grave

Symbolic of the cruelty and pain I gave

They called me a liar, scoundrel and a cheat

I made enemies of everyone I'd meet

Somehow, someway, someone pulled the cord

No one shed a tear or spoke a kind word

Symbolic of the cruelty and pain I gave

Many black roses lay on my grave

Stories

There are many stories new and old through the years always being retold

Chilling tales that make your blood run cold

Rarely are they believed, yet I have seen dreadful things unfold

If you too witnessed such horrid events a hand you would seek to hold

You surely would quiver and shake, never again would you stand bold

In the stillness

Darkness surrounds as clouds cover the moon

You feel a chill about what will happen soon

Hope has vanished with the absence of light

Now you are left alone with the uncertainty of night

Underneath

In tunnels deep beneath the city

There is another world below

Strange creatures lurk in silence

There is so much that you don't know

They plan, they plot, and they scheme

When they attack there will be nowhere to go

You will try to run and try to hide

They will catch you, you're too slow

She

She walks the streets of the city, her face covered in a long black veil.

She waits for those who will call her name, what it is I'll never tell

She comes when called with moans and screams, hear her wail

She finds you no matter what; your hair turns white and skin pale

She pulls you into the shadows she calls home, there you will dwell

A Storm is brewing

Dark changes are on the way

In the blowing wind the trees sway

The rain won't wash the pain away

Like thread I begin to fray

Alone in the eye of the storm I lay

Break in

Was that the front door creaking open?

I hear a stranger's voice, words spoken

Someone is now in this house with me

I peer around the corner to see

The intruder is a beast of black light

Stupidly I yell out in terror and fright

All the shadows then take human form

I'm lost in the dark once they start to swarm

My Pet

Deep inside the shadows is where I lurk

Keeping watch and waiting as I see my master work

In the corner against the wall sits her broom

The steam from her cauldron rises to fill the room

My yellow eyes glow bright in the increasing dark

For a moment all is silent, nothing heard, not even a lark

A laugh cuts through the cold night air

If she sets her sight on you, you'd better beware

One Night

Carelessly buried deep in the ground

A murdered woman can be found

One day a storm was raging in

Strange powers would even this sin

The killer was at his normal game

He had a girl cornered, when she came!

She grabbed his arm, breaking the bone

He was buried by his victims, he was not alone

Command

You hear my voice; listen to it, without question

Walk across the room, and up the stairs, go!

My hold on you is more than an obsession

To the window, on the ledge and down below

Lady in Waiting

Oh, I pulled her corset strings tight

With all my strength and might

Breaking her ribs, crushing her lungs

From her eyes blood runs

She fell to the ground

Lifeless on a priceless rug her body was found

Zombie

The dead have come to play

Up from their long sleep

In need of flesh they crave

Until sunrise they will stay

Slowly behind you they creep

You know you cannot be saved

They are banished by sun's rays

Back to the ground, where they will keep

When they return try to be brave

A Night Time Fright

You ran to the car in the parking lot with a fright

Dropping your keys, in the darkness they are out of sight

A soft voice speaks, "Too bad the sky is not bright"

A shadow slowly turns to you, a knife reflects the light

The last thing you saw were those eyes, now all you see is night

The Midnight hour

Glass jars full of skin, teeth and hair

A boiling cauldron and an empty, creaking rocking chair

The magical spells she reads fill the air

What she is doing is more than I can bear

When Morning Finally Comes

They wait until dawn when you feel most safe

They are not bothered by the morning light

When with the sun you breathe a sigh of relief

They are in the bushes hidden just out of sight

As you walk to work not suspecting a thing

They leap upon you with surprising might

They scratch and bite and tear you to shreds

Through the pain and shock you try to fight

They overcome you, you've lost too much blood

Take this as a warning, it's safer at night

Shut in Tight

I awake to see shadows and a glimpse of moonlight

I cannot escape this wooden box, I try with all my might

I hear dirt thrown on top of me and wonder, is this all just spite?

I no longer see the moon, covered in earth, I now know true fright

I hear an unknown voice shout, "Sleep well, goodnight!"

Watching

Behind the thin curtains made of white lace

I see a figure, with burning eyes, a lifeless face

Slowly the ghoul comes at a haunting pace

The Underworld

Nyx, she is the bringer of the night

The one who gives the shadows life

Painting the sky with a mist dark

Charon, he is the seeker of the souls

All that are lost follow him to the river of Acheron

And there they hear Cerberus bark

The Erinyes, a group of three ladies whose whispers

Drive you into a down spiral, a demented state

You are left a shadowy stark

Hades, he is the underworld god who imprisons all he wants.

Few have escaped his clutches and those who do bear his mark

Wicked Roots

There is a mighty tree that grows alone

Where nothing dares to grow in its sight

Its branches are thorned, thick, and knarled

Those who see it are filled with fright

No nests or hives have ever been formed upon it

It does not die with snow or grow with sunlight

It stands in its own ominous glory

Do not question or harm it, it can handle a fight

Welcome to the Party

In the middle of the night you hear a shout

Thinking you were alone your mind is filled with doubt

Another scream comes from a dark hall, you follow the moan

The room you are in is unknown to you, a chill tingles each bone

Now shaking you force yourself to take another step

Your ears are met with a shriek like death

Your heart pounding, you walk through the door

There a lifeless body lies, in the corner there are four

You see a figure in black with a knife in hand

Death comes quickly in the killer's signature brand

Lost

Late in the night I walk the streets alone

You may sometimes hear me cry and moan

The movement outside your window is me

By the time you notice it is too late to flee

The light in your eyes and all hope is gone

You are paralyzed by my haunting song

Bloody Mary

Say her name three times slow

A Silhouette in the mirror starts to glow

You are unable to flee from this terrible foe

Now the blood and scars start to clearly show

Stepping through the mirror, she shrieks like a crow

Her powers are something you dread and know

She leaves behind another victim, the legend will grow

Night Terror

In the moonlit sky a menacing bat flies overhead

It comes through the window, eyes glowing red

Taking human form it stands over your waiting bed

Swiftly you are bitten, devoured, drained dry, left for dead

Hunger having been satisfied, it leaves fully fed

Once again it takes to the sky, filling all hearts with dread

Now to the place that it dwells, it walks the halls among the undead

In a satin-lined coffin, it closes the lid without a word said

Shadows coming

Deep in the shadows, I hear a voice calling out to me

I stand in shock; it repeats my name one, two, three

The shadows take shape of a fiend, it brings me to my knee

Wicked

The unholy witching hour will be upon us soon.

A caldron boils, stirred slowly with a spoon.

"One more thing, an eye from a blind raccoon".

Her black heart is like a storm, a raging typhoon.

Into the night she goes wearing a cloak, like a cocoon.

A broom flies across the haunting silver moon.

Her victim will not hear the clock chime come noon.

The Full Moon

A cry pierces the frosty midnight air filling your heart with fear

Echoing howls resound through the sky with a haunting eerie sound

Traveling in a pack they are all around now watch your back

The way is lit by a silver moon beam, petrified you cannot scream

On and on you run, they take their time, this chase has only begun

You trip on your untied shoe, looking up you see yellow eyes watching you

They belong to a massive hairy beast filled with hunger longing for a feast

It lunges at you in an attack, you feel its fangs then all is black

In the Night

In the middle of the night I awake from my sleep

All is dark and silent, I hear not a peep

I feel something stirring; see it across the bed creep

It drags me down into the abyss, dark and deep

The Voice

You hear a voice in the night calling, calling

Into madness you are falling, falling

The voice gets louder still calling, calling

Into nothingness you are falling, falling

A Chilling Tale

In my mind there is a void, my heart is heavy

My hearing is acute and my eyes are fine

Doctors could not find anything, yet I know I am not well

Time has aged this home and robbed me of my youth

My Victorian palace has a past unknown

I can find no peace in this place where I dwell

No colleagues dare to visit; tensions and emotions are too high

My once beloved home has made me an island unseen

All alone, I am trapped inside this silent prison cell

When the moon is awake my home becomes alive

A Chill in the Air: A Collection of Stories and Poetry

I am alone, yet I hear others rushing through my home

In the dead of night when I sleep I hear them yell

I lie awake in growing despair as my mind wanders

The others who came before me suffered fates I dare not speak of

They whisper in my ear, their stories they long to tell

Gothic tales of terror, grief, and dismay

I could spend my life writing these terrifying stories

A book so unbelievable, it would never sell

My parlor is their playground, my piano plays on its own

My rocking chair creaks as it rocks back and forth

All my possessions hanging on the wall, all at once they fell

Sandlin

In anguish they await for daylight's break

Soon, once again night will fall; I will no longer be alone

These walls hold in the haunting spirits, my home is their shell

A storm brews, ominous and cruel

They are awake, sweet revenge is what they seek

My fears ring loud and clear like a haunting bell

Their voices call to me louder, drawing me near

With a fast-beating heart I draw my last breath

The house and I are now one, I never need say farewell

A Chill in the Air: A Collection of Stories and Poetry

Twisted Tales

A Chill in the Air: A Collection of Stories and Poetry

The Garden

Lucinda Harris was a lady that lived on the outskirts of town. Her home was well suited for her aristocratic life style. Though the year was 1950 she preferred her dresses, furs, pearls and hats from the turn of the century that she wore in her youth. Now that Ms. Harris was in her seventies she needed help in the garden she loved so dearly. A young man named Fred Wilson answered the ad and was hired. Since he was new to town he was the only one crazy enough to work for Ms. Harris. As I said Lucinda Harris was an aristocrat that believed in the ways of her past. Rumors about her were spread like wild fire. Fred was to work for her Monday, Wednesday, Friday and every other Sunday. The hours would be few and the work would be easy once he got a good start.

The first time he saw the garden he couldn't believe it. The ivy that grew along the tall brick fence was grey, all the flowers were black and white, frozen in time, as they looked to be in bloom. The grass was brittle and brown. The trees were wilted and the fruit that grew on them was rotten. He started by clearing out the flower beds and cutting off all of the dead branches. The next work day he watered all the plants that looked like they could be saved and the grass as well. Then on his next day he trimmed the ivy, only leaving what had a little life in it and pulled all the bad fruit.

Over the next few weeks the garden was growing thanks to Fred's hard work. The trees gave fruit, the ivy was as green as ever, the flowers were in bloom and the grass was green and lush. As the garden continued to flourish Fred became consumed by the thought of this green paradise. His visits grew longer each time, until he never left. All he did was tend to the garden day after day. All while Lucinda Harris watched from her window. After some time Ms. Harris put out another ad. It seemed her hired hand went missing. While she waited for another young man, she tended to the garden the best she could; thankfully Fred gave the garden life again. Some will tell you that if you walk by you will see an odd tree whose bark swirls in, making it look like the face of Fred Wilson. But if you want to take a closer look, you must ask Ms. Harris nicely.

The Haunting at Dara Mor

The year was 1909 when newlyweds John and Agnes McCormick were given a home and land deed as a wedding present from an unknown guest. They packed a picnic and took a motor tour to find their new home. After nearly two hours they found it.

John spoke out, "This can't be right!"

It was a large brick home, much like a manor house, on its own little hill, surrounded by Irish wildflowers. Agnes reread the address four times before proclaiming, "This must be it, John!"

After having lunch they walked the land, deciding the property and land were too big for just the two of them. They invited his bachelor brother and her unmarried orphan sister to come live with them. They packed all of their belongings and within two days they were all moved into the house.

Monday morning John traveled back to the city for a week of work. Patrick had agreed to be their groundskeeper and Agnes and Sarah decided to breathe new life into Dara Mor.

As Patrick was clearing the field he heard a voice call out to him.

"Excuse me!"

He stopped his work and looked over to see an older man who looked to be about seventy.

"If you don't mind me asking, what are you doing here?"

"My brother and his wife are the new owners and I'm their groundskeeper." Patrick replied.

"I'm Duncan Roger, I'm the only neighbor you have. I've been here since I was a young lad. Dara Mor has been barren for fifty years for a reason." then he was on his way.

Patrick knew how superstitious people could be and thought nothing of it.

Agnes and Sarah were cleaning the parlor, dusting the walls, scrubbing the windows, and mopping the floor. "I already know that we will all be very happy here!" Agnes proclaimed.

After many hours of work, all of them retired for the evening. Though there were five bedrooms, Sarah and Agnes refused to sleep alone.

A whisper awoke Agnes from a sound sleep. She spoke, "Sarah, did you say something?"

Sarah did not reply so Agnes went back to sleep.

A few days went by as normal. Agnes and Sarah were now ready to hang the wallpaper while Patrick started to plant the garden. The day was rather hot and Agnes and Sarah had the windows open. They heard a knock and were both brought back to a time of ghost stories. Agnes whispered, "That was a knock on the door."

Sarah looked to Agnes, "Aggie, this is your house, answer it."

Agnes looked brave, "I will, but you need to come with me."

The two sisters went to the coat hall, and tried to see who was behind the door, peering through the stained glass. They couldn't tell who it was. Agnes realized she was being silly and opened the door. There was Duncan. "Are you Mrs. McCormick?", he asked.

Agnes ran her fingers through her red wavy hair, "Yes,

You must be Mr. Roger, my brother-in-law Patrick said
you two met the other day."
Sarah smiled, "I'm Miss MacMillian, but you can call me
Sarah."
He did not seem to care much about her, "Mrs.
McCormick, I wanted to let you know that when I was
young I was the groundskeeper for the Albright family
that lived here, and that the small wooden building on the
far right of your land means a lot to me. Please don't let
anyone go in there."
"I don't see why we would need to, it's so far and we have
plenty of room in the barn. Consider it yours." Agnes said,
"Would you like some tea?"
"Good day." he said and walked away.
Sarah and Agnes looked at each other "How odd," Sarah
said. "Why would you agree?"
"We don't use it, and we never will, so if it makes an old
man happy that it is still standing why bother?"
They went back to preparing the room.

Friday evening came and John was back at Dara Mor,
Agnes and he were in each other's arms, soon he drifted
off and she was trying to sleep. In the complete darkness
she saw a green light that barely shined through the key
hole. She went to see where it was coming from. As she
reached for the knob the light vanished. "My tired eyes
must be playing tricks on me.", she said softly so that
John would not hear. She laid down again and this time
quickly fell asleep.

In the morning Sarah and Agnes made breakfast for
everyone. Soon after Patrick went to show John what
work had been done, and also what he needed John's help

with. Agnes and Sarah thought they should skip the dining room for today to clean and paint the porch.

"Sarah, come here!", Agnes called out with joy.

"What is it?"

Agnes pointed to the bottom of the wall, "Children must have lived here!" There were little animals and two houses, one was Dara Mor and the other looked like Duncan's house, painted at the base of the wall.

"They're not very good." said Sarah.

Agnes looked at her in offense, "They are charming, and much better then what I've ever been able to do."

"Very true," laughed Sarah.

Agnes looked confused. "Why didn't we see these before?" she asked.

"Oh, Aggie, they are so small and at the baseboard. We haven't had time to look for children's drawings," Sarah answered.

"Maybe you are right, Sarah, just be sure not to paint over them. I do like them." Agnes smiled.

Sarah interjected, "Today after some work, let's go to Mr. Roger's home and ask if he knew the children."

Agnes was glowing, "I like that idea!"

A few hours passed and the ladies took a break to make some goods for the neighbor they wanted to impress.

Later that evening Agnes and Sarah went for their walk to Mr. Roger's home. In a basket they had soda bread, jam, some goat cheese and apple cider. Agnes knocked on the door and they waited. About a minute later Mr. Roger opened the door.

"Oh, hello Mrs. McCormick,"

"I don't know if you remember me, I'm Agnes' sister, Sarah."

"Can I help you Mrs. McCormick?", he asked impatiently.
"My sister and I were hoping to see your home and we
have this basket full of things for you."
"Thank you, but I am very busy at the moment." He took
the basket and began to close the door.
"Oh! One minute, Mr. Roger."Agnes said. "I was
wondering, who were the children that used to live at
Dara Mor?"
"There were no children."
"Well, that is curious because there are little pictures
painted on the porch wall just above the baseboard."
"That is curious." he said and closed the door.
As the sisters walked back Agnes said, "I suppose the
drawings must be older than we first guessed. These
children would have left before Mr. Roger came here. I am
truly glad we found them. I feel they are a part of the
house. I just wish I could know their story."

The next day after church, Agnes saw that the children's
pictures were painted over. "Sarah! Sarah!" Agnes called,
wondering what could have happened.
"Yes, Aggie?"
"Why did you paint over the drawings? You know that I
was planning on keeping them!"
Sarah looked utterly confused, "Aggie, I didn't. I know
how charming you found them."
"Well, someone did!" Agnes said.
"Who would do that? You could tell we left them alone."
Agnes looked to Sarah, "I'll ask John and Patrick."
After asking both of the men and both knowing nothing of
it, she realized that she was losing her mind and must
have painted over them herself.

Then came Monday and John had to return to work. Sarah went into town to see her friends and Patrick went back to his parents' home to help out, leaving Agnes alone until Friday. She spent all of Monday staining the staircase, polishing all the wooden furniture in the parlor and dining room and finishing her work by painting the little table that belonged to her mother a lovely shade of green. After all the hours of work without nearly any breaks she curled up in the large chair that John always sat in. She soon fell asleep with the smell of his pipe lingering in the fabric.

When morning came the sunlight poured into the room, shining on her face. She went to the kitchen and had a small meal then made her way to the staircase as she needed to get a new dress from her room. She stopped in her tracks with a scream. Her eyes fixed on small hand prints of green paint on the stairs. She broke into tears, "What is happening to this house?" She ran to the top of the stairs, only to be pushed back by a violent gust of wind. She grabbed the banister. Panic filled her heart. The wind stopped and she slowly finished her way up the stairs and into her bedroom. She opened her jewelry box and took comfort in her rosary beads. "Dear God, bless his house!" she cried out.

The next day Agnes only did house work and spent all her spare time by the small pond, reading her books of Irish Poetry. She found some peace in her kitchen making candies, pies and cider. All of Thursday was spent in there, hopping these goodies would make her family feel welcomed. As she took some time to play her piano she was overcome by smell of fresh paint. "Where is that

Sandlin

coming from?" she asked herself. She walked into the dining room where she saw Dara Mor painted on the wall. She was in awe, then the piano started to play. She ran into the parlor where nothing was happening.

That night after she was ready for bed she heard whispers by her door.
"Come on Kate, come on George." she heard clear as day.
"Enough is enough!" She yelled out, storming to the hall here she saw the green light again. It darted to the top of the staircase and she followed it down to the foyer and into the kitchen where it vanished. She shook her head, her red hair moved like a million candle flames. She needed a glass of water and light for her lantern to light her way to the well. As she entered the kitchen she saw a woman in a long plaid dress sitting at the table with three children, a girl about eleven and two boys nine and seven. They laughed as they drank their tea and nibbled on their poppy-seed muffins. The table was lit in a rose colored light. Agnes found this scene peaceful, forgetting that this was her home. All at once the light changed to green and they were only inches from her. Their faces were elongated and grey and their eyes were black. They screamed, "Out!"
Agnes fell to the floor as the nightmares melted away.

Friday came. John, Sarah and Patrick returned to Dara Mor. They found Agnes working in the garden. She smiled and gave them all the treats she made. John and Patrick were happy to find her in such a good mood, although Sarah could sense something was wrong with her sister. John and Patrick found the painting of the home and both praised Agnes for her secret talent. Sarah however knew that Agnes could never have drawn it. That night Sarah asked Agnes to help her mend a dress hem. Agnes walked into Sarah's room, "Well, where's the dress?" she asked. Sarah walked to the door and closed it, "Agnes, sit down." Sarah told her pointing to the bed.

"Sarah, is there something wrong?"

"Yes, Aggie there is!" Sarah held her hand. "You're acting so odd, as if you have no emotions. What happened when we were gone?"

Agnes whispered, "Sarah, I don't want John and Patrick to think I'm mad! I'm not crazy like Mother."

"Aggie?" Sarah spoke with tears in her eyes. "What happened? You need to tell me so I can help."

Agnes curled into her little sister's arms, "Sarah, this house hates me. It makes me see things, things no one should see, I don't know what I can do."

Sarah held her tight, "Aggie, maybe you are just tired and you need my help. I'm sure you will be fine after some rest with John at your side."

Agnes soon fell into a deep sleep and Sarah left to tell John that Agnes needed him. He found his sleeping wife and carried her to their bedroom.

In the middle of the night Agnes woke to find that John was where she needed him. She tried to sleep but couldn't, "Perhaps some tea will help." she told herself, hating the idea of walking through the house at night. Yet she fought her fear. When she closed the bedroom door behind her she heard voices from Sarah's room. She ran to help her sister not knowing what evil might lurk there. She flung open the door to find Sarah and Patrick talking of marriage. "I'm sorry." Agnes said softly. "I heard voices and I was worried."

Patrick laughed, "No need. Sarah and I are just talking."

"Yes, I heard." said Agnes.

Sarah and Patrick looked at each other and smiled. Sarah turned back to her sister, "This May, we will be married and we will be sisters and sisters-in-law!"

Agnes rushed to them and hugged each of them. Soon she left and made her way to the kitchen where she made tea. She was unworried for the first time in awhile. She had her cup ready and when the pot started to whistle she turned to the stove and saw the steam in the shape of a child's face. She dropped her cup and it shattered as it hit the floor. She just sat on the floor with no words. The steam soon faded and her eyes flooded with tears. Hours later John came into the room and found Agnes just sitting there. "Agnes, what's going on?" She didn't answer. He ran to her and lifted her up. He carried her into the bedroom where she fell asleep.

Agnes awoke to see Sarah's face, "There you are Aggie! You had all of us worried."

"What happened to me?" asked Agnes weakly.

Sarah's smile faded away, "We don't know. John just found you in the kitchen early Saturday morning."

"What day is it?" asked Agnes.

"It's Thursday." Sarah started to cry, "I didn't think you would ever wake up."

Agnes looked to Sarah, "I'll be fine, but I need your help."

"Anything, anything at all, Aggie!" Sarah kissed her sister's hand.

Agnes and Sarah were soon dressed and went for a walk to their neighbor's home.

Agnes pounded on the door, "Duncan Roger!" She repeated over and over again as Sarah shouted out "Mr. Roger!"

Finally he came from around the side of the house on his large gray horse. "What is your problem, Mrs. McCormick? Why are the two of you yelling like banshees?"

Agnes bolted to the horse and took the reins in her hand. "Tell me who is haunting my house!"

Sarah stood at her side.

"Let go, Mrs. McCormick." He pointed his pistol at her. "Don't think I won't shoot!"

"Sarah!" Agnes shouted.

Sarah took out her gun and pointed it at Duncan. Time stood still as the Irish wind blew cold air on their faces. Duncan was the first to speak. "Ladies, you need to go home."

Sarah spoke, "Drop the gun and we'll leave."

He did and they left without a word.

Back at the house Agnes was ranting.

"Sarah, I know that he knows what is happening. He knows who the family was and he knows what happened to them!"

They heard a loud thud, "That came from the attic." said Sarah.

The sisters went up the stairs and to the door that lead to the staircase that would take them up to the attic. Once in the attic they found a strange metal box with Dara Mor painted on the lid. Agnes took the box and they went downstairs where she opened it. Inside were photographs of the woman and children that she had a vision of in the kitchen.

"I wonder who they were?" Sarah said.

Agnes started to cry, "I've seen their faces before. They are the ones who haunt this house."

"Aggie, are you sure?" asked Sarah.

"Yes."

Then another thud was heard, this time from the kitchen. They both went to see what it was. They saw a rolling-pin on the floor. The door opened and the rolling-pin rolled out to the porch and down the stairs. They followed as it continued to pass the garden and the pond, into the field and finally to the little shack Duncan Roger was so worried about. The rolling-pin stopped instantly as did the girls who had chased it for nearly five acres.

Agnes opened the door. They found that the floorboards were all gone.

"Why would someone remove a floor and keep the building standing?" Sarah asked.

Agnes looked at her sister, "Mr. Roger is hiding something here. We need a few things."

They returned with shovels and a lantern. For hours they dug through the dirt until Sarah said, "I hit something." They got on their knees and started to move the dirt with their bare hands. They both fought not to scream as they saw a skull.

"It's her." said Agnes.

"The mother?" asked Sarah.

"Yes."

Then a voice shouted out from the distance, "Who's there?"

"That's Mr. Roger." said Sarah.

Agnes turned out the flame in the lantern. "Go to the house."

They moved like the wind. Once inside they barricaded all the doors and windows that they could. Soon after they heard knocks at the door.

"Let me in, Mrs. McCormick!" yelled out Duncan, trying to break in.

"Let's hide in the attic." Sarah whispered.

"Alright." agreed Agnes.

They hid well, behind a large beam. Screams were heard and thuds followed. Shrieking echoed through the home. Sounds of glass breaking and metal bangs filled the air.

"Be gone you unearthly beasts!" was the last thing they heard Duncan cry out.

The two fell asleep and by morning they heard John and Patrick calling out to them.

They rushed down the stairs and into their lovers' arms.

"Oh, John I was so scared!" cried out Agnes as Sarah held Patrick.

"I didn't know if I would ever see you again." she said with a deep breath.

John held Agnes at arm's length, "What did you do to Mr. Roger?" he shouted.

"What are you talking about?" yelled Sarah.

Patrick then held Sarah in the same manner, "Duncan is dead in the dining room. His head was removed from his body, which was shredded apart." Agnes slapped John, "How could you?" she blurted out.

He hit her back, "You are crazy and so is your sister, just like that mad Mother of yours."

The next day Mrs. Agnes McCormick and her sister Ms. Sarah MacMillian were found guilty for the murder of Mr. Duncan Roger and were both put into the custody of St. Helena's hospital for the criminally insane, where they lived out the rest of their days.

The Mystery of Marie

It was a cool October day just like any other until I saw a brewing storm was about to hit. I took a quick shower knowing that I had enough time before it did. When I stepped out onto the bath mat blood started to drip from my body. Slices were cut into my flesh everywhere. I blacked out.

I awoke in the bathroom; I was dressed in a red dress I'd never seen. Standing, I realized my skin was uncut, looking into the mirror all seemed fine, aside from the mystery dress. I heard a voice calling my name, "Marie!" I turned around and I was outside. My home was gone! I was completely lost.

"Run", I told myself, and I did. I ran fast and I didn't stop until I reached a dilapidated train depot. I looked at the broken pieces of glass, and saw a reflection, but not mine, the reflection of Morgan, my mother! Then from nowhere a stinging pain burned my side.

With a scream I woke. I was tied to a bed covered in white linens, and white walls surrounded me.
"Calm down, honey. It was just a shot." said an older woman, a nurse.
"Why am I here?" I asked.
She smiled. , "Let's not talk about it again, Morgan."
"Morgan!" I cried out, "Morgan is my mother. I'm Marie, Marie Russell."
The nurse left the room, but I could hear her talking to another nurse. "That poor sick woman, she still thinks that she is her daughter. "
"Well, where is her daughter?" the other one asked.
"Oh, she killed her nearly ten years ago. Marie was taking a shower, when she sliced her up with a knife."
"Marie!" I yelled and yelled until finally I drifted off to sleep.

The Girl Next Door

Cole Anderson stared out the window of his 3rd floor apartment. *What am I even doing here?*, he wondered. Three years ago he had graduated college with a history degree. He had yet to do anything with it. Immediately after graduating he moved into this plain brick Seattle apartment building that looked exactly like a dozen others he passed every day and got a job at the local furniture store. He felt as if his life was wasting away and there was nothing he could do to change it. Here he was, Twenty-five years old and he had not accomplished a single goal he had set for himself.

He took a deep breath; there was nothing he could do about it, no sense in being late for work.

As he was getting into his car, he saw Millie Hayes, the old woman who lived in the apartment directly below his, sitting in her car with seemingly no intention of leaving any time soon. Mrs. Hayes had a habit of sitting where she thought no one could see her and watching the neighbors. Sometimes he felt bad for her that she didn't have a better way to spend her time. But if he was being honest, there was something about her that he found unsettling.

He waved to her and she stared past him as if he were invisible. He turned the key in the ignition and nothing happened. He tried again, the engine came on, and loud music filled the car. He hit the power button quickly and relaxed a little as he was met with silence once again.

Work was long and tiring, sometimes the stupidity of people astounded him, and when he pulled into the parking lot at 7:30 he was happier than he could ever remember to see that boring, old building in front of him. He started the coffee pot and looked in the refrigerator, then the freezer, then the cabinets. He had forgotten to go shopping. Again. He was just about to leave when he heard a scream from next door. He didn't even know someone was living there. He ran out and knocked on the door. A few moments later a beautiful woman about his age, with long ash blonde hair and sea green eyes, answered the door.

"Hello?" she said questioningly in a thick accent he did not recognize. "May I help you?"

He looked past her and saw nothing that seemed out of place, the living room was very orderly and neat and there was a movie playing on the TV. "I heard a scream and wanted to make sure you were alright. I'm Cole Anderson." He reached out his hand to her.

"I am Sabra Barrow." she said, ignoring the gesture, "and I am quite alright. I have just been sitting at home watching a movie. That must have been where you heard the scream from."

"It must have been. Well, it was nice to meet you, Sabra. Hopefully I'll see you around here."

"Yes, we must spend some time together soon." She sounded bored. "I must be going now, I have a lot to do."

"Okay, I'll see you later."

She closed the door without replying.

When Cole got back from shopping he realized that he had left the coffee pot on. He ran into the kitchen and saw it sitting there emitting a steady stream of smoke with the burnt remains of coffee in the bottom of the pot. He turned it off and put the pot in the sink, he would deal with it later.

There was something different about Sabra. He couldn't stop thinking about her. Sure, she was beautiful, but it seemed like there was something else about her that continually drew his mind back to her.

Hours later as Cole tried to sleep he heard another scream pierce the air. He looked over at the clock in surprise, it read 3:17. What was she doing watching TV this late? He pulled the pillow over his head and tried to shut out the noise.

The next morning came too early. As he headed out something caught his eye and made him go back to Sabra's door. In the carpet right in front of the door was a small blood stain. He knocked on the door. This time Sabra opened it immediately.

"Oh, hello there, Mr. Anderson." she greeted him cheerfully. "To what do I owe this unexpected visit so soon after the last?"

"Please, call me Cole." He said. "I noticed this blood stain outside your door and wanted to make sure you were alright."

She smiled, "That is from this morning when I went to get my mail. As I was opening my letter I got a paper cut and must not have seen the stain. Thank you for letting me know, I will clean it up before it becomes permanent."

Cole smiled, "You're welcome, I'm just glad you are okay."

She smiled again, a cheerful, radiant smile. "Your concern for me is quite endearing."

He blushed slightly, "It's only what anyone else would do in this situation. What are neighbors for, right?"

"Right, well, I must be going now, perhaps we will meet again soon."

"I'd like that."

That brief conversation with Sabra brightened Cole's day significantly, he didn't even mind that one customer changed his mind 6 times on which dining room table he was buying. The best part was that with this new attitude, he sold twice as much as he would have in a normal day.

However, as he made dinner that night, he heard yet another scream, and this one sounded way too real. He started to doubt if Sabra watched as many movies as she claimed to. This was crazy, how could such a bright-eyed, beautiful, sweet spoken young woman do what he was thinking. His lack of sleep must be playing with his mind. Still, something felt wrong.

He remembered to check the mail and as he was walking back he saw Millie returning home.

"Mrs. Hayes," he said running up to her. "how have you been?"

She stared back at him with russet brown eyes that rarely seemed to blink. Every time Millie Hayes looked at him, Cole had a feeling that she knew everything about his life, all of his failures and shortcomings, and that she judged him for all of them. "Be a dear and skip all of the pleasantries and just tell me what you want."

Momentarily offended, Cole tried to find a way of asking about Sabra that didn't sound insane. "Do you know anything about Sabra Barrow?" He finally asked. "She just moved in next door to me and...well..." he struggled to find the proper words, "there have been some concerns from recent events."

"Use plain English please, what has you so worried about this new girl? Do you think someone wants to hurt her?"

"No. Well, I really don't know. I have heard a few screams and seen some blood, but she always has an explanation for everything, the TV has been on so that should explain the screams and she claims the blood was from a paper cut."

Millie's demeanor completely changed, she seemed more interested now. "Well, if that explains it, why have you come to me?"

"Because something still feels wrong. The screams sounded very real and that was a lot of blood for a little cut."

"And you want me to what, spy on her for you?"

He realized how stupid all of this sounded. "No, of course not. I just wanted to know if you had seen anything strange. I don't want anything bad to happen to her."

"If the girl says she is fine, then I would guess she is fine. It's best to stay out of other people's business."

He almost laughed at this coming from her. "I guess you're right, thank you for putting my mind at ease." Nothing he could have said would have been farther from the truth. Now he had the feeling that Millie was lying to him too. He began to suspect that he may actually be insane. Isn't this how they always said it started, with paranoid delusions of strangers? Still exhausted, he decided to go to sleep early in hope that tomorrow would be better.

The next thing he knew, the door was creaking open. Glancing out the window he saw only darkness. Had he left the door unlocked? In a panic he searched for anything he could use as a weapon. He ran to the kitchen and opened a drawer. Before he could pull out a knife a force struck him from the side. He soon realized it was Sabra. In the dim light she looked like a ghost, blonde hair and bright eyes almost glowing. She pushed him against the wall and to his surprise, no matter how hard he fought, he could not get free. *This must be a dream,* he told himself, *your insanity has crept into your sleep now.*

She smiled at him, like a cat playing with its food, "I heard you have been asking questions about me, and that's just not acceptable. We can't have anyone finding out who I truly am. So, even though I like you and had hoped to keep you around a little longer, it is time for you to go."

Before he could ask what she meant, she opened her mouth to reveal long, sharp fangs. The last thing he heard was her wicked laughter ringing in his ears.

The Tub

Her eyes fluttered open; once she was fully awake she started to panic. Her voice was contained as I stuffed her mouth with a rag and duct taped her lips together.

I loved the mix of anger and fear in her big brown eyes. Her hands were bound with a scarf I had gathered from her closet. Her legs were tied with her pantyhose. I placed her in the porcelain tub. She flinched each time her skin touched the cold white porcelain.

I turned on the hot water; it started to fill the tub. I watched as she tried to get free, but there was no way. The scalding water was raising and grayish-white steam was filling the air. Her skin was now red. I nearly boiled her alive; all that was left was to hold her down. I pushed down her head; her blonde hair clung to my hand like seaweed.

I was done and able to live my life without her.

Vanity

There once was a young woman with eyes that shined like sapphires in the sunlight, skin like a rich December snow, and hair as black as midnight. She was the belle of the ball and the toast of the town. She had all the materialistic things anyone could wish for. Her flaws could not be seen by the eye, only by those who could feel her looking down on them.

One day to her surprise a large crate was delivered. More surprising was the fact that it came with no note. No sign of who may have sent this large gift to her. She demanded that her servants bring it inside at once. When they had opened it she saw the most beautiful vanity in the world. It stood two feet tall and six feet long, made of ivory, with a three foot tall mirror. The mirror was framed in an ornate heart design, and ivy and cherubs were etched into the ivory base. At once she had her old oak vanity taken away and burned to make room for this new treasure.

She sat at her new vanity hour after hour, watching herself closely as if she was watching a great actress in a stage performance. Brushing her long locks of raven hair, painting her china face and adorning herself with shimmering jewels; trying to hide the bitterness of her soul and the emptiness of her cold heart.

That night as she dressed for bed to her horror she saw that her reflection was delayed. To make sure it was not her mind playing tricks on her, she ran her hand across her mirror. Nothing peculiar happened. She picked up her silver brush and started to brush her hair. She then finished with her nightly ritual, which included applying lotion to her alabaster skin and admiring herself for a moment. Once she was in bed, she was awoken by strange cries and voices whispering. She laid there petrified until sunrise.

The next day she once again sat at her beloved vanity to prepare herself for the day. Trembling she saw that all seemed to be fine. When she finished with her powder puff and started to paint her face, she gazed at herself in the mirror. Her reflection's skin began to chip off her face like an antique painted doll. Her flesh was gray, and her eyes sank in as if she was a sickly and aged woman. She frantically rubbed the mirror as if it was fogged. The glass shattered across the room cutting her skin. The blood splashed and stained the entirely white room behind her. Now with her flesh ripped away and her blood streaming down her body, she began to weep like a young child. Looking to her treasured mirror to see the damage done, she found that the mirror was gone and all that remained of it was the hollow frame. A monstrous hand appeared and reached out, grasping for her face, she screamed as the hand quickly pulled her in.

One of her mistreated maids came in moments later with the silver breakfast tray. All she found was a blood-stained white fur rug, pieces of broken glass and a diamond bracelet on the edge of the spoiled woman's vanity. She laid down the tray, walked over and put the bracelet in her pocket. She then walked way and called for the master of the house.

The Henley House

It was the end of senior year, and we were about to graduate. Knowing that our summer would be full of working and making plans before going off to college, we decided to do something a little crazy.

There was an old house on Riddle Drive that we had been avoiding since we were little and first heard the stories of it being haunted. We decided that it would be fun to stay there for one night; spend some much needed time together and put a silly old rumor to rest. We grabbed some sleeping bags, flashlights, and enough junk food for an army.

Our little ring was just like any other, there was myself: the "Goody-goody", my boyfriend, Cameron: the all-American golden boy, my cousin, Lily: who we all called "Wildflower", Jackson: the sweetest guy you'll ever meet, Skyler: our residential prep, and Matt: the one who always just wanted to be free.

We all came in through the back door so we wouldn't be noticed. We looked around and saw empty cans on the floor, dust caked onto every surface, and so many cobwebs that the rooms felt about half their size. The floorboards made a creaking noise that echoed through the house. Out of nowhere thunder began to boom and lightning cracked across the sky. Hard-hitting rain collided with the roof.

We set up in the living room that was full of chipped and cracked decorations.

"Are you sure we should be here?", I asked.

"Come on, Maggie, where's your sense of adventure?" Cameron joked.

"I guess you're right," I said uneasily. "It's just one night, what could happen?"

After we sat there for a few moments in silence, Lily said, "Are we actually going to do anything, or are we just going to sit here staring at each other?"

"Good point," Matt said. "I'm going to go see the rest of the house. Anyone who wants to join me for the grand tour is welcome; the rest of you can just sit here and play it safe like Maggie."

We each grabbed a flashlight and joined Matt. He switched his on and led us into the dining room first.

The entire house appeared to be frozen, trapped beneath layers of white dust and gray cobwebs. It looked like it had been forgotten for decades. I brushed the dust off of a small crystal bowl and coughed as it swirled through the air around me.

"It's a shame everything was left here, these must have meant a lot to someone at one time," Skyler said.

"These look really old," Lily said, walking over to a sideboard where there were several bronze zoo animals. "Even compared to everything else. I wonder how much they are worth." She picked up the elephant and put it in her bag.

In a way only Jackson could, he put his hand on Lily's shoulder and said, "I think we both know that you should put that back."

With a mixture of anger and embarrassment she did.

"Maggie! You won't believe the books in here!" Skyler exclaimed.

I followed her voice into an amazing room with ceiling-high bookcases lining the walls.

Skyler held up a pristine copy of *The Great Gatsby,* "It's a first edition; the binding on this book is older than my great-grandma!"

"I wonder what other books are here." I was interrupted when we were called back into the living room by Cameron.

"Okay everybody, Matt here has decided to try to freak us all out by telling the story of Beatrice Henley."

"The year was 1950 when old man Henley was 63 and he made 16 year old Beatrice his bride. She was a poor girl and her starving mother was more than happy to trade her in for a few dollars. Beatrice didn't know what to do when she moved into this big house which was older than the city itself. So she got a maid, a woman from Ireland named Mollie O'Leary. Mollie had been working for the old man and his child bride for about two years, when he died. After that Beatrice became the toast of the town, her parties were like no others. She was called the happiest widow on Riddle Drive.

Mollie stayed with Beatrice, until one day she broke the lady's best punch bowl. Beatrice stabbed her in the heart with one of the jagged pieces. As Mollie fell to the ground, trying to pull out the glass, her last words were a Catholic prayer. Beatrice flew into a panic, "Where should I hide the body?", she asked herself repeatedly. Then an idea struck her, "I'll hide her in the walls of the attic." she said out loud, laughing at her own brilliance. After removing a few wooden boards, she placed the maid into the wall and sealed it shut, never to be opened again. If we were to go upstairs right now and pull out the boards, we could still find the remains of poor forgotten Mollie O'Leary. For years the seniors of Graymont have searched for her and never been seen again. It is believed that the ghost of

Beatrice Henley still guards her secret today and kills anyone who dares try to unearth it."

"Ooh, what a scary story", Cameron mocked.
"Go ahead and prove me wrong then." Matt challenged.
"Is this really necessary?" Skyler asked.
"If you're afraid, you could always stay down here alone." Matt said.
Skyler didn't answer. Cameron and I led the way, followed by Lily, then Skyler, who was reassured by the fact that Jackson would be right behind her. When no one was looking Matt closed the door behind us.
We found five doors. As a group we moved to each door, opening them to see what we could find. The first door to the left led to a small bedroom, the second for another bedroom, the third to the master bedroom, then the fourth door took us to yet another bedroom, finally we went to the last door to find that it was locked. Jackson and Cameron tried to open it with no luck.
"Let's just go." said Skyler.
Then the floorboards started to creak. We all entered a state of panic. We were standing still, then I felt someone's breath blow across the back of my neck, and a hand rested on my head. I screamed, Lily and Skyler joined in as Cameron and Jackson started to ask what happened. The glow of all our flashlights started to move out of control.

"Calm down", said Matt with a laugh, "I can't believe all you freaked out."
"That's not funny, you loser", said Cameron as he pushed him.

Matt kept laughing, "You better watch out or Beatrice Henley will get you."

"Leave Maggie alone." Jackson said. "I think it's time for us to all go downstairs now."

He led the way and we all followed. Once I was at the top of the stairs I looked back and saw that the door was closed but I didn't mention it because I knew Matt was just trying to scare us again. No one spoke until Jackson reached the door and turned the knob. He must have thought the door was stuck because he tried again.

"That's really not funny, Matt.", Lily said. "You have the key right?"

"I didn't lock it.", Matt said, looking slightly disturbed.

"That's enough Matt," Cameron said, "Now unlock the door."

"I'm serious guys, I didn't lock it. I closed the door to scare everyone, but I made sure it was unlocked."

"Yeah right," Lily said. She was about to say something else when she stopped. "Where's Skyler?", She asked with genuine fear in her voice.

She wasn't with us anymore.

Matt laughed, "Alright Skyler, I get it. You're mad at me for scaring you and you want me to worry now. It's not going to work so you can come back now."

We went back upstairs and couldn't find her.

"Skyler," I called out. "If this is a joke please come back now, I'm really worried."

No response.

Lily spoke out, "I'm trying the door again." She ran across the hall and down the staircase. I was right behind her. On our way down the guys still called out for Skyler. Lily and I finally reached the door. We tried so hard to get out.

Lily started to cry, something that never happened. I held my cousin close.

Lily and I went back upstairs to where the guys were still checking the rooms.

"There's no point," ,Cameron finally said. "She's not here anymore."

"Then where is she?" Lily asked.

I looked around the room, this couldn't be right. I lifted the flashlight again and slowly moved the beam of light across the room again. "Is Jackson still checking the rooms?"

Matt and Cameron left to look for Jackson, I could hear them yelling his name as they walked through the rooms. Lily must have also gone to look because she wasn't next to me anymore. Her location was soon known by a loud scream. I ran into the first bedroom and found Lily on the floor sobbing. As I moved closer to her I saw him. Jackson laid in a pool of blood; his throat had been slit open. We all stood there in horror and no one dared to speak. It felt like years passed. This night had started out as a big joke, a bunch of friends just goofing off together. How could it end in death? What was happening here? Finally Matt was able to speak, "What do we do now?", he asked quietly.

No one knew how to answer. We knew we had to get out. Someone else was in here with us and they were playing with our minds. I ran to the window and looked down, there was no way of climbing out, just a straight drop. Matt, Cameron, and Lily quickly ran to check the others. Cameron took me in his arms, "I'll keep you safe, Maggie". I had nothing to say.

As we stood there Lily's flashlight went out. A moment later I shone mine where she had been standing. There was an empty space. Now we were down to three.

Our blood ran cold as we heard a thud in the master bedroom. Cameron said, "Matt, keep an eye on Maggie while I go see what that was."

"You know I will." Matt replied.

As soon as Cameron left, Matt came over behind me and put his arm around my shoulder.

Cameron returned quickly and paused for a moment before saying, "It was Lily."

"Is she..." I couldn't bear to finish the question.

Cameron walked over and wrapped his arms around me. Matt stood off a short distance looking hopeless.

"We need to come up with a plan." Cameron said, sounding determined. "No more splitting up, we need to watch each other's backs. Only one flashlight on at a time, we don't know how long we will be stuck up here. We know the killer is using the master bedroom, so we will have to wait there."

"So, your master plan is for us to go wait to die?" Matt asked.

"We don't have any other choice." I spoke up, "There are three of us. At least we have a chance if we stay together. The killer doesn't know that we figured out where they are coming from. Maybe we will have surprise on our side."

Time stood still, as we just waited. We spoke very little. There was a noise from the other room. We all just stayed put, until the noise repeated. Cameron said, "I will stay here in case anything else happens. Maggie, please go with Matt to see what that was. You will be safer together."

Against my better judgment I went. The room appeared empty when we got there. As we were about to leave I noticed something on the floor. I walked over and picked it up. It was the first edition copy of *The Great Gatsby* that Skyler showed me earlier. Matt held something out to me. It was the bronze elephant Lily had taken.

"The killer has been watching us every moment since we have been here."

A look of horror crossed Matt's face, "They are just distracting us."

"What?" I asked.

"Cameron."

We ran back to the master bedroom but it was too late. There was no body, just blood, way too much blood. I knew Cameron was gone.

Matt held me, "I'm so sorry." he said. I knew then that he wanted to kiss me, but he wouldn't out of respect for his best friend. But I wasn't that strong. I kissed him and then laid my head on his shoulder and closed my eyes out of complete exhaustion.

I was awoken by a small glimpse of the morning sun. For a moment I forgot where I was. Then the memory of last night hit me like a ton of bricks. I looked around for Matt and finally saw the back of his head as he sat in a chair. I walked over and kissed the top of his head. He slumped forward and fell off of the chair. Blood poured from the deep cut in his throat. I sat there sobbing as I realized I was all alone now.

"Come on, there's only one left now," I screamed. "Let's finish this already!" I didn't care if I lived or died anymore. All of my friends were gone.

I heard a faint knock coming from the wall and slowly walked towards it. I knocked in the general area that the sound had come from. Two loud knocks echoed throughout the room. My attention was drawn to thin lines cut in the wallpaper in the shape of a large square. I stood there quietly until I saw the bottom line start to rise. Soon I was face to face with an elderly woman.

"It is time the truth was heard." she said.

I took a step back. I didn't know what else to do.

"Crazy they called me, a killer they all whispered. Everyone got it in their mind that I killed sweet Mollie O'Leary and stuffed her in the wall." she went on, "Nobody ever minded to ask what really happened. Do you want to know, well, do you? She ran off and got married! That's all. Ever since 1955 all these brats broke into my home. My home! On a dare. Well, if everyone wants me to be a killer, I don't want to let anyone down." She finished with a laugh and ran towards me.

I ran as fast as I could, down the stairs and to the door. I began pounding against the door, desperately trying to get away. I turned to see Beatrice at the top of the stairs. She slowly, deliberately, took each step towards me; enjoying my helplessness. She smiled wickedly as she reached the last step.

Dancing the Night Away

On a balcony a dashing man in a suit and a ravishing lady wearing a black backless dress dance as the golden-pink sun shines behind them, highlighting their faces. Soft music fills the jasmine perfumed air. Around and around they twirl about. He holds her close and whispers sweet nothings in her ear. She tells him about her hopes and her dreams, and that he is one that is coming true. For hours they seem frozen in time. Her heart is lighter than ever before. As the moon starts to awake his hands become gray and his fingers are elongated with nails a foot long. He digs into her back, pulling down and across. He is tearing her apart. Blood covers his monstrous hands. They continue to dance until she is hollow, her limp body falls to the floor. He composedly cleans his hands and returns home. Waiting for another invitation.

A Night at 7D

Three days after I received news of my grandfather's death, my only cousin, Sam, and I went to grandfather's apartment to sort through his belongings. We were chosen for this because we were the only ones able to travel to Liverpool at such short notice. I had just quit my job as a waitress at a small diner and Sam's work as a writer made it possible for him to travel whenever necessary.

The apartment building was surrounded by run-down shops, and made from the same deteriorating red brick.

At the front desk sat a woman with grayish-red hair barely held in a bun, who was wearing a plain, pale green dress. She had a tired look on her face.

Sam told her, "We are John Everson's grandchildren, I'm Sam and this is my cousin Annie. May we please have the key to room 7D?"

"Sure, let me fetch it," She said with a tone of contempt. "I'm Mrs. Delton, I run this fine establishment. If you need anything I'm sure you can find it on your own, you look capable enough."

As we headed toward the elevator she shouted, "The elevator is out of order, use the stairs!"

We finally reached the 7th floor and it appeared to be deserted.

When we entered the apartment we felt a sudden chill. Sam tried to turn on the heat, but the thermostat was broken, so he said, "We are going to have to deal with a cold night."

It was odd for us to walk into our grandfather's apartment, as we had never been there before. We did not have much contact with him when he was alive, because he was mad at our parents for moving to America when we were young.

"Do you want the couch or grandpa's old bed?" I asked.

"You go ahead and take the bedroom," he replied.

I took my bag into the room and found that it was full of boxes. I yelled to Sam, "We better start now; this is going to take a while."

We each grabbed a few boxes and took them into the living room. Sam opened the first box and found that it was full of papers and letters. He looked around and said, "These walls have so many stories to tell."

I smiled, "So, you're still a writer?"

"I am a published author," he corrected me, jokingly kicking my foot.

"Yes, I know. You were published four years ago, what have you done lately?"

"Are you still a waitress, Annie?" he asked, changing the subject.

"No, not anymore," I answered. "A year of waitressing was enough."

"So, how many jobs is that now?"

"Well, there was waitress, librarian, dog walker, personal shopper, and freelance singer/songwriter." I answered, counting them off on my fingers.

"What does that mean?"

"No one bought my music."

Then I came across a photo album, on the last page was a photo of a small gathering. I was surprised when I saw that the man at the far left looked like a recent photo of our grandfather.

There was a knock at the door. Sam went to answer it as I pulled out the photo to see when it was taken. It was unmarked so I placed it on the coffee table and went to see who was at the door.

There was a man standing in the doorway, he had black hair and dark eyes. There was a mysterious charm about him.

He said, "I'm sorry to bother you, but I haven't seen John in a few days, is he alright?"

"He died, so he's not doing too great." I said.

"Oh, I'm sorry, have you contacted the family?"

"We are the family," Sam said. "We are his grandchildren. I'm Sam, and this is Annie."

"Well, as long as everything is alright, I guess I'll be going. By the way, I'm Ted Lewis, I live at 7G, come get me if you need anything."

"It was nice to meet you, Ted." I said.

Sam closed the door and said, "I didn't think anyone else lived on this floor."

"Me either." I said.

"It's too cold, I'm calling maintenance." Sam picked up the phone and immediately there was another knock at the door. I opened it to find a man in green overalls with a nametag that said, "Frank". There was a touch of grey to his brown hair.

"I'm here to fix the thermostat," he said.

I was completely surprised and asked him, "How did you know it was broken?"

"I know the building, it's my job."

After tinkering with it for a while he said, "I'm sorry kids, I will have to come back later and see what I can do."

After Frank left, Sam saw that it was 11:50pm.

"We'd better get to bed," he said, "Grandpa's funeral is pretty early."

I awoke not much later from an extreme heat. I looked around and saw the room was full of smoke. I started to cough, made my way back to the living room to check on Sam, and was shocked to find out that there was no smoke.

Sam came out of the bathroom and asked if something was wrong. I explained what I had just seen.

"It must have been a dream," he said, walking towards the bedroom. "I will make sure everything is alright." He came back a moment later and said, "There isn't any smoke in there."

There was a knock at the door. I looked at the clock. It was midnight; who could this be?

When Sam went to see who it was, I couldn't help but hope it was Ted. It was a young boy in tattered clothes. He was a fair child with blue eyes, around the age of six.

"Help me." He said in an eerie voice.

"What's wrong?" Sam asked.

Once again he said, "Help me." His voice echoed.

"How are we supposed to help you?" I asked. "Tell us what to do."

Then we heard a woman yelling, "Timmy, where are you?" Then she appeared, also in old clothes. Her dark hair covered most of her face. She picked him up and ran down the hall. We watched as she ran, and they vanished.

"You saw that too, right?" I asked Sam. He guided me back into the apartment and said, "Calm down, we will figure this out. You can sleep on the couch, and I will sleep on the floor next to you."

I woke at 2:00am and made my way to the bathroom. When I was done washing my hands I turned around; the bathtub was filled with water. I yelled for Sam and he came running in. "How do you explain that?" I asked, pointing at the bathtub.

"It could have been dripping this whole time," he said, sounding unsure. He pulled the plug out and went back into the living room.

I followed and said, "I'm calling a taxi. I can't stay here, this place is haunted!"

"You're over-reacting," he said. "This place is not haunted!" Then, all at once, all of the pictures in all of the rooms fell to the ground, shattering the glass.

"Are you okay?" I asked when I saw the frightened look on his face.

"I'm fine." He answered.

When I gathered myself, I took the phone to call a taxi. The line was dead. I got my bag and pulled out my cell phone. It wouldn't turn on. I went back to Sam and found out that his phone was dead as well.

Then all of the lights began to flicker, the windows all opened, and the water began to run. A moment later all was still. One of the boxes in the center of the room opened. Sam walked over to see what was in the box. "It's full of newspaper clippings." He said.

"What do they say?" I asked.

"I don't know, I just looked in the box." He took out the first clipping, the headline read, "Apartment Fire." He was silent as he read.

"What's wrong?" I asked.

"What was that boy's name?" he asked slowly.

"Timmy, the woman was yelling Timmy."

He held out the paper and I read, "The only two unable to escape the fire were Rebecca Jones and her young son, Timmy." I took it from him and continued reading to find that they lived in apartment 7B. I ran to the door of 7B and knocked. The instant my hand touched the door, it turned to ash. I screamed and turned to find Ted standing there.

"What happened?" he asked.

"Either something is going on, or Sam and I are both going insane."

"Let's go talk to Sam." He said.

As we came back into grandfather's apartment, Sam looked towards me and saw that Ted had come in after me. "Get away from my cousin!" He yelled.

I ran to Sam's side and asked, "What's wrong?"

"He's dead! Here, look at this. He died in a car crash in 1995." He held out an obituary with a recent picture of Ted. As soon as he saw the picture, Ted vanished.

I fell to my knees, "What's going on, Sam?"

"I don't know, Annie."

"The picture!" I exclaimed suddenly.

"What picture?"

"The group picture," I exclaimed, taking it from where I left in on the coffee table. I pointed him out, "That's grandpa."

"And that's Rebecca and Timmy," he said.

"You're right," I said looking at the rest of the picture, "There's Ted."

There was another knock at the door. Sam motioned for me to be quiet. "It's Frank, I came back to fix the thermostat. Sorry it's so late."

I found his obituary in the box and slid it under the door.

"What's this?" he asked. Then silence.

I knew what had happened, "He's gone," I whispered.

We finally got the courage and ran downstairs. I ran to the front desk and said, "I need a taxi. Tell Mrs. Delton I'm not coming back, do whatever you need to with the apartment."

The man at the desk said, "Mrs. Delton? She has been dead for 20 years now."

"Is there more than one Mrs. Delton? I saw her just last night."

He pointed to a photo, "Is this her?"

"Yes."

"It couldn't have been her. She is dead."

"Of course she's dead. Now can you call that taxi?"

As he picked up the phone to call the taxi, he added, "There are rumors that the 7th floor is haunted."

Finally the taxi arrived.

Now safe and on our way to a hotel, I looked at Sam and smiled.

"Why are you so happy?" he asked.

"I'm just glad we're okay, I was so worried about your heart."

"My heart isn't that bad, cousin."

"That's not true; you couldn't play sports in high school."

The taxi driver asked, "Are you saying something to me?"

"No," I responded, "I'm talking to my cousin."

"Oh, are you on the phone?"

"No," I said, looking at Sam and laughing.

He was not smiling, "Annie, ask him how many people are in the backseat."

Then my heart dropped. I told Sam, "I don't want to ask."

"Ask the driver, Annie."

"Excuse me," I asked, my voice shaking slightly. "How many people are in the backseat?"

"Only one person as far as I can tell," he laughed.

When I turned to look at Sam he was still there which

gave me hope. Then he smiled and said, "I love you, Annie." and vanished.

The Girl in the White Dress

The year was 1915 and I had just turned 19. I went for my
morning walk like always. In a buggy passing by I spotted
a young vision with red flaming hair and eyes golden-
brown like the wheat. She was wrapped in a white gown
made of lace. My dreams were of her that night. She stood
on a grassy cliff leaning on a willow tree, her flaming hair
and the white dress blown by the crisp air.

The next time I made sure to be at that same spot at the
same time hoping to see her angelic face again.
I waited for hours, finally leaving after realizing this was
not her pattern. I went home to start my work. That night
I laid in bed when I saw her form eclipsing the moonlight
shining through the window. I was taken back; as she got
closer I woke, regretting the end of the dream.
The next few days I was visited by these delightful
dreams, how I wanted to see her again!

Until one night I was awoke by terrible pains coming from
every fiber of my being. My room seemed to merge with
another that had candles burning and women chanting.
My body soon turned to sand and I faded into nothing.

The red headed girl looked to her mother and sisters,
"Perhaps, the prayers will work and the haunting dreams
will stop."

Evening the Score

I awoke to a blinding light. "Where am I?" I asked myself. Then I noticed I was tied to a chair "Hello! Hello!" I yelled out. I couldn't see beyond the shining white light.

Something hit my head and I was out again. This time I awoke and I saw a room that was made of concrete. I was freezing cold. The lighting was dark and there was nothing I could see that would help me to know where I was. I then noticed I couldn't move my lips; there was something in my mouth.

It was cold and hard, like glass. Then I heard a noise, it must have been a door opening, because now I was not alone. "Hello," an older lady said as she came face to face with me. Her grey hair framed her dry, wrinkled face. "Do you remember me?" she asked.

I made a few muffled sounds as I tried to plead for my life.

"Oh, that's right you can't talk much right now can you?" she smiled. "I'm Mrs. Dundee, you lived two blocks away from me when you were a small boy; remember the little brown house on the corner of Travis Street?"

I remembered, and I knew what she was about to do.

"One day you came to my house with your baseball bat and broke all my lawn animals: my sweet deer family by the oak tree, my circus elephant in my flower bed and my bears in the middle of the lawn by the bird house. You threw rocks into my windows, breaking my lamps and vases and little statues my mother had." She started to cry, and then after a few minutes she wiped her tears. "My neighbor Viola told me it was you! But then you moved away."

I thought to myself, *I was wrong; I was just so upset that we had to move, I wanted to destroy other people's things, I didn't know any better, I was only six.*

She started to laugh as she stroked my hair, "It only took me thirty years to find you." She pulled out a chunk of my hair, leaving behind a bleeding scalp. "That day you did that to me I was at the hospital with my dying husband and daughter who were in a car crash, and after they both passed I went home to find everything was broke, including that circus elephant they got me for mother's day."

She took out a box from underneath a small table, "Here are a few things your parents left behind. As you have noticed one of your mother's glass jars is in your mouth." She pulled out a screwdriver, "Your fathers!" she jammed it into my eye. Blood was everywhere and I could barely scream thanks to the jar. Then after some time, I saw from my other eye that she had my mom's old pan, "Wonderful. Cast iron!" she said as she hit me in the side of the face, shattering the jar within my mouth. The glass cut my tongue and shredded the inside of my cheeks; I swallowed at least five teeth.

"Please let me go!" I cried out.

"You had this coming!" she yelled. "Here is a bag of marbles you left behind." She stared to beat me with them; I could hear my bones cracking with the blows.

She then showed me a wire hanger. "From your parents' closet!" she took the dull curve and with much force she started to stab me with it. As I started to bleed out, I heard crinkling; she was filling the basement with paper. "It's a shame all the paperwork, birthday cards and school papers you folks left behind. From what I could tell I was in a sea of paper and blood. She said one last thing, "Good bye!" then closed the door and I smelled fire.

Painted Wings

The year was 1862. Little did I know everything would change that fall I turned 16. I was soon to marry Cyrus, but none of us knew what would unfold. I was so sheltered by the little town of Behrmont, Maryland. I never ventured too far into the forest that nestled us. I always thought we were safe until blood was spilt on that unassuming day.

The sun rose that morning the same way it always had. I started my chores as normal and was hanging the clothes to dry when Beatrice Davis, my dear friend who lived next door, came over to tell me the terrible news. Bea's eyes were red and she could barely breathe, "The Morrisons, the Morrisons, all of them are gone! All slit open like animals and left to bleed out!"

I was shocked to my very core, feeling a pain I had never known.

"W-Who..." I took a moment to breathe before continuing, "Who would do that?" There had never before been violence in our little town and nothing made sense anymore. We both cried as the clothes swayed in the wind.

Later that night we met at Father's church. All of the families in Behrmont were there. No songs were sung, no flowers were cut, just a few hours of silence, and four wooden crosses that bore their names. It seemed that everyone hoped this would be forgotten, but how could it be so easy? Good people were murdered. Would there be others? This is what we all wondered.

Later that night I had a few things to do, as Mother was sick and getting worse, and Father could not seem to speak or move much after the services. I was cleaning

around the smokehouse when I heard a whisper. "Dolly."
It called my name, and once again I worried, *am I next?*
Then a hand touched my shaking shoulder, it was Cyrus.
"I didn't mean to scare you, Dolly."
"It's alright, I just worried you were..."
He then held me close, "Don't finish that thought, we will
be fine."
I was comforted for a moment but I somehow knew that
this could not last. "They're still out there, Cyrus," I
whispered. "Whoever did this is still out there and they
might come back. How can you be so sure we are safe?"
We stood there in each other's arms, listening to the wind
for a time before we said our goodbyes.
The question was answered all too soon. It had been three
days since the terrible deaths of the Morrisons and once
again bloodshed fell upon our little town. People began to
realize that this was not going to go away if we simply
ignored it.
It was more dreadful than the last. The father and mother
- Joshua and Louisa Foster were found suffocated with
large masses of cotton spilling out of their mouths, their
children - Hiram, Elsworth, Lawrence, Francis, Julia, and
Richard were all found scattered throughout the house
and front yard, full of bullet holes. The youngest seven
children - Kenneth, Betty, Andrew, Pamela, Albert,
Donald, and Amy were simply left to drown in the well.
Their eldest daughter, my friend Flossie, was found the
next day in their cornfield, her head split open and her
blood staining a large rock.
The largest funeral that I ever saw was held the following
day. Soft whispers could be heard throughout the church.
Things like, "Will this happen again?", "Who's next?", and
"Why?, was uttered the most.

Father and the other few men left in the town held a
meeting at our home to discuss the goings on; they were
unaware I was listening. George Whitaker, our town's
sheriff and Cyrus' father was among them.

"We all need to stay alert," he said, "The Morrisons and
Fosters unfortunately lived on the outskirts of Behrmont,
we live much closer and are able to watch out for one
another. Never leave your children unattended.
Remember, stay civil, but do not trust anyone."

My uncle, Morton Allen, spoke up, "Maybe it is time we
leave Behrmont and move to a larger town."

"My family cannot give up our land, it is our livelihood."
Beatrice's father stated.

"We all need to calm down," Sheriff Whitacker said, "We
know David Morrison sold cheap lumber and cheated
many people."

Then my father spoke, "But Joshua and Louisa were the
salt of the earth, who would kill them and their fourteen
children?"

I could no longer bear to hear the arguing so I ran outside
to get some water for Mother. I heard Beatrice call my
name and saw her standing in her garden.

Bea told me, with tears on her face, "Father said that until
things are resolved, I'm not allowed to leave the yard
anymore." Her voice grew more depressed. "What if my
family is next?"

I gathered all the courage I could and told her, "Don't
worry."

She looked me in the eyes and asked, "Aren't you scared?"
I took her in my arms and answered, "I'm petrified."

Then Bea's mother called her in and I made my way
back home through the small field.

Sandlin

A few silent days passed, then in the dead of night I was
awakened by the smell of smoke. From my bedroom
window I saw the Davis' home engulfed in
raging scarlet flames. In my nightgown I ran through the
field. I tried to enter the front door, to no avail. I ran to
the back. It too was barricaded. I ran to each window, only
to find that they had been boarded up for their protection.
The flames grew higher and the house started to cave in.
I felt arms around me, pulling me back. The next thing I
knew, I woke up in my bed. Across the room Father sat
in a chair smoking his pipe, and Cyrus sat next to him,
looking at the floor. My Aunt Lydia laid a cool, wet cloth
across my forehead. She looked down at me, kissed my
cheek and said, "I can't tell you how happy I am to see you
open those beautiful brown eyes."
I cried out, "She's gone! Beatrice is gone, isn't she?"
My Father made his way across the room, he ran his hand
through my hair and whispered, "I'm so sorry, my sweet
girl."
"What are we going to do?"
No one answered. We sat there in thick silence that was
full of fear and loss.
"Father," I finally said, "can we have the funeral as soon
as possible so I can move on with my grief?"
Father and Aunt Lydia were both lost for words. Cyrus
came to my side and said, "We have already decided there
will be no funeral. There is no easy way to say this... there
was nothing left but bones and ash."
I flew into a rage and started breaking everything in sight.
I screamed, "Why Bea? Why her?"
Father got a tight grip on me and pulled me to the ground.
I cried for hours.

We just sat there for a long time before I looked to the back of the room where Cyrus had been standing. "Where is Cyrus?" I asked, my voice still shaking.

Before Father could answer, Cyrus returned, looking more scared than I had ever seen him.

"What happened?" I asked.

"We have to leave now. I know no one wants to go, but now we have no choice."

"We would have already left if that was an option," Father replied sadly, "we have nowhere to go."

I took Cyrus' hand and looked into his eyes, "Tell me what happened."

"I'm sorry," he took a deep breath. "it's your Mother's sister Lydia and the family... they're all gone, Dolly."

"Gone!" I screamed. "Why is this still happening?"

Father left us to tell Mother that her only sister passed on.

"How did they do it?" I asked.

"That's not important." he answered as he held me close.

"Tell me."

"Your Aunt Lydia and cousin Roberta were both hung from the oak tree. Your Uncle Morton was found with his head severed. Jacob and Meredith were locked in the smoke house and it was set on fire, and little Samuel was found in the stream after he had been shot."

I was unable to speak or move. This was just too horrible for words. I sat there sobbing as Cyrus held me. Then I summoned all of my courage and stood. I took a shaky step towards the door.

"What are you doing, Dolly?" Cyrus asked.

"I am going to find the person responsible for all of this."

"I understand you are upset, but you cannot go out there alone."

"Then come with me."

"There is nothing we can do," he said. "all I care about anymore is keeping you safe. Please do not leave this house."

"I'm sorry, Cyrus. I am done sitting here doing nothing. I have to leave or I will go crazy."

"I can't let you go! You need to be here with your Mother and Father, you are their only child who made it through the fever that killed half of the town ten years ago. Besides, I'm far too selfish to let you perish. I need you, think of the children we'll have."

I held him and lied, "Go get your family and Father will marry us today, then we will all leave tonight." I kissed him for the first time. He kissed me back and left without saying a word. I gathered a knife and my Father's small gun, placed them in a leather bag and left a note. "You will all be saved. I'll take care of this, somehow, some way." signed, "Remember me, Dolly."

I knew whoever had done all of this must be hiding in the woods, so I set out in that direction. As I passed by Cyrus' home I knew something had changed. I didn't see anything unusual and was about to keep walking when I saw something glistening from the corner of my eye. There was a small red splatter on the front window. My heart pounding with terror and dread, I opened the door. Nothing could have prepared me for what I saw.

Mr. and Mrs. Whitaker were both left on the floor with axes in their chests, Clara and Peter had been impaled with pitchforks, Amos appeared to have been beaten with a shovel, and there was a saw splitting Tabitha's head open. The worst was Cyrus, shot, the barrel of the gun stuck in his mouth, where only minutes before my lips were. I could not believe it, was my betrothed Cyrus the killer? Did he know that he would soon be caught? Why did he kill himself?

I ran and ran, into the woods. I screamed out hateful things and birds fled from the safety of their trees. I became lost in time. As the moon lit the sky I began to walk home.

The chaos in my mind calmed as I gazed upon the most beautiful creature I had ever seen and dropped my leather bag. A majestic blue butterfly with golden specks, brighter than I had imagined possible fluttered before my eyes. It led the way and I followed without question. My mind was no longer my own. It seemed like I had been walking for hours and yet no time at all had passed. This waking nightmare now seemed as only a distant dream.

The next thing I knew I was standing over my Mother's dead body holding the pillow I had just used to smother her. I turned; there in the corner of the floor was my Father in a pool of blood, his straight blade razor run nearly through his neck. Then all at once I stood on a cliff looking down at a body of water. That beautiful butterfly floated by and I jumped.

The Sunburn

Have you ever had a bad sunburn? Well, this is the story
of Donny Finley and the worst sunburn he ever had.
It was a hot July day and Donny Finley and his girlfriend
Julie went to Myrtle Beach to swim and relax in the
Carolina sun. Julie was wise and lathered with the sun
block, which Donny didn't bother with at all.
"I'll be fine!" he said while stretching for a swim.
"Alright, but I don't want to hear you cry when you get
burnt."
"I never burn!" laughed Donny.
The rays beat down on Donny as he slept in the golden
light and Julie spent the time in the water. After getting
out she saw his skin turning red and thought she would
teach him a lesson. She let him continue to sleep while she
left the beach for lunch and some light shopping.
After some time the beach filled with a crowd of people,
the noise of laughter and many small portable radios
woke him. As he opened his eyes he let out a little gasp.
He looked at his arm, it was red as blood, everything was
red. Even with the slightest movement he felt great pain.
After flinching a hundred times he managed to sit up. He
didn't even bother to gather his things he just wanted to
get to the hotel and soak in cold water. He walked three
blocks, passing by people that pointed and gasped.
Including people saying "Look at the poor man" or "That
is why we use sunscreen!" and a little brat that said
"There's Mr. Lobster" Donny wanted to frown but he
knew it would hurt too badly.
Once he got to the hotel he took the elevator of course. He
went into the room where Julie was watching TV. "Oh,

Donny I'm so sorry!" Her face looked terrified, "I never imagined, you would burn so badly"

He looked at her and said "I'm going to take care of this don't bother" he went to the bathroom and locked the door.

Seeing his reflection, he couldn't believe how much worse he looked in the bright lights. He could hear Julie outside at the door about to say something when he started the bath water. He soaked for hours, feeling some relief, when he got out he dried off only to find the towel was covered in flakes of skin. He kept drying and more and more dead skin fell to the ground. Then like a child he started to pull the skin off, he was amazed how quickly it happened. Nearly eight hours went by and Julie knocked on the bathroom door. There was nothing. She knocked again. Again there was nothing. She called the manager and explained what was happening. He came with a key. Once the door opened all they saw was a large pile of dead skin.

Never Trust a Stranger

It was a cold December night four years ago. It was just another shipment of plywood from New Jersey to Illinois, a trip Patrick Robinson had made many times before. The blowing snow caused the sky to become seamlessly white. In a semi covered in a sugar-like glow sat Patrick, an average Joe. He had sandy hair and hazel eyes. He took a sip of his piping hot coffee as the steam warmed his otherwise frozen face. A drop of coffee spilled onto his blue flannel shirt. He turned the dial on the radio as his favorite old country song started to play.

He spent miles alone on the frostbitten roads. All of a sudden he spotted a small, red car pulled over to the side of the road and stopped to see if they needed help.

He saw a woman through the nearly frosted over glass. She had long, wavy blonde hair; a smile beamed ear to ear as she saw a friendly face.

As she rolled down the window, revealing her features the moon lit up her calm blue eyes. She shouted out, "My cell phone's dead and if I can just get to Pennsylvania my sister can come get me."

"I'm headed to Illinois; I can drop you off on the way.", He said.

"Thank you, it's hard to find nice people anymore; most people wouldn't have even stopped."

They drove for a few minutes, not saying much. She introduced herself as Gina Adams.

"So, what's your sister's name?" he asked.

"What sister?"

"The one who is supposed to meet you in Pennsylvania." He said in confusion.

"Oh, right. I meant my cousin. But I was raised by my Aunt Jean so she is more like a sister. Her name is Marissa. What's your family like?"

"I'm married to a great woman, her name is Allison. We

have two kids, a boy and a girl. Jenna is six and Toby is about to turn four."

"Aw, those are cute names. So, do you come from a big family, Patrick?"

"I'm one of six." he said.

"How nice, I always wanted a big family."

They rode for a while longer, each sharing a few stories about their lives. Morning came; the golden sun brought new life to the snow covered hills. They pulled over for gas and a few things to eat.

As he finished pumping the gas he found Gina standing a short way off, looking down into a valley. She yelled out, "Hey, come check out this view!"

He made his way over, looking into this beautiful winter view. The tree tops were covered in snow and a frozen stream ran through the snow covered valley.

As she stood next to him she said, "You know, Patrick, I'm really glad I found you."

"Well, I'm just happy I was able to help you out." He replied.

"You can't trust everybody anymore."

"There are still some good guys left."

"You wouldn't believe how many people would just kill for fun."

Then, with unexpected force, she pushed him down the hill. He laid on his back, looking up, wondering how he got there. Then his eyes widened in terror as he saw that this once helpless woman was now a knife wielding lunatic. She laughed. He tried to get up and she kept laughing. She was laughing so hard that she was now crying. He stood up.

She said, "This would be a lot more fun if you ran."

The chase was on; all she had to do was follow his footprints in the snow. He came to the frozen stream, he had to run across it or be caught. He desperately hoped it would hold his weight. He ran across it in a flash. His heart beat faster with each cracking noise that he heard. He kept running until finally he leaned against an old frost covered tree. He tried to catch his breath and closed his eyes. He was thrown back into reality when he felt the sting of a cold blade enter into his side. He once again heard that evil laughter. She pulled out the blade and rammed it into the center of his chest and slowly pulled down until she reached his waist. As he took his last few breaths she whispered into his ear softly, "Poor, Patrick, didn't anyone ever tell you? Never trust a stranger."

There he laid, all alone in the blood-soaked snow. Gina was now on the main road. She was crying. Her thumb was in the air, hoping someone would stop.

A young woman pulled to the side of the road. As she rolled down her window the brunette asked, "Are you alright?"

"No," she replied. "My boyfriend and I got into a fight and he told me to walk rest of the way to Illinois."

"What luck!" the woman replied. "I can take you to Ohio; I am going there for my parents' anniversary."

"That would be perfect." Gina replied.

The brunette let her in, saying, "I'm Nora."

"It's nice to meet you, I'm Patricia."

The Great Outdoors

It was June 15, 2015 and we had just graduated high school. We each had plans to go to college at different schools, so we decided to plan one last trip before we had to leave. We packed up and headed out to the lake for a weekend. It was me, Niki Rosewood, the nerd of the bunch, my best friend Michael Griffin who was almost as nerdy as I was, the twins Ava and Audrey Clark who couldn't be more different - Ava was preppy and studious while Audrey was popular and liked to play dumb, even though both of them graduated a year early, Jeremiah Reese, Audrey's boyfriend who none of us liked, and Aria Matthews, our fearless leader who took charge of the group when we were younger.

The weekend promised to be interesting at the very least. We decided to kick off the first night with a campfire and ghost stories. Aria, naturally, went first.

"It was in these very woods twelve years ago that Sarah and Thomas Whitefield decided to camp for their honeymoon. It started out wonderfully, the sun was shining, the birds were singing, all was right with the world." Aria paused to comment, "So obviously something horrible has to happen next, right? A storm started brewing. Darkness fell over the woods and the air grew dense. Strangely there were no nighttime noises. There weren't even any birds fleeing from the storm. Thunder began to boom and lightning struck. Sarah and Thomas held each other close and waited for it to all be over as rain collided into the side of their tent. Then they heard a scraping noise coming from the ground underneath them. Thomas told Sarah to go wait in the car while he found out what it was. As soon as she was gone Thomas started pacing in panic and fear. He knew this had to be what he had done a year ago coming back to haunt him. As he took another step a hand reached out of the ground and pulled him into the shallow grave below."

Ava gasped and Audrey grabbed Jeremiah's hand. Jeremiah just laughed.

Aria continued, "The ground moved immediately to swallow him and there he remained to pay for the crimes of his past. A short time later Sarah went to check on Thomas, and all she found was his favorite old hat laying on the ground."

"You call that a scary story?", Jeremiah mocked.

"Well, why don't you tell a better one then?" Aria challenged.

"Sure.", he replied confidently. "Enough of these tall tales and ghost stories, why don't I share the true story of this place?"

"Go ahead." Michael said.

"In the spring of 1992 a man named Daniel Davison was wanted for murder. He knew that if he was found he would never again be free. So he ran. After driving for nearly eight hours straight he found a large forest. The trees were twisted and gnarled and grew close together. He knew that even if they came here looking for him it would be easy to hide and nearly impossible to find him. A year passed and he grew restless. He started walking around the forest at midnight, looking for anyone foolish enough to enter his territory. Knowing that he would need a place to bury the bodies, he cut down a section of trees, creating this very clearing we are sitting in right now. Time passed and truth became legend. This place became a very popular camp ground. And that is how we came to be here right now."

My voice was quiet as I asked, "What happened to Daniel?"

Jeremiah grinned, "Most think he died, others think he left. Me, I think he's still here, waiting for his next kill."

Audrey looked upset, "That's not funny, Jeremiah. I think I'm done with stories for now."

Aria smiled sympathetically at her, "I think that's a good idea. Let's all try to get some sleep."

We all woke up in the middle of the night to a high pitched scream. I ran out of my tent into the clearing and looked for a sign of a struggle. There were no sounds and the clearing was empty except for me, Ava, Aria, Jeremiah, and Michael. We all looked at each other in fear as we silently asked the same question, where was Audrey?

"That was her." Jeremiah said. "Audrey was the one screaming. I'm going to go find her."

"Let's be smart about this." Michael said. "We don't know what's out there. I will go with Niki and Ava to the right, and you can go with Aria to the left."

Everyone agreed that this was a good idea and grabbed the flashlights and went to look for our friend. I don't know what it was that made me decide to pull out my phone and check the time, but it sent a chill through my spine when I read 12:06. I showed Michael and he said, "Let's hope this is just a sick joke." his voice didn't sound like he believed it though.

I heard the leaves rustle and saw movement out of the corner of my eye. I got Ava and Michael's attention, and silently pointed. Michael took my hand and we waited. A moment later Ava smiled, "It's just the wind." she looked somber as she added, "Come on, let's keep looking."

An hour passed, still no sign of Audrey. Ava started to cry. she sat down and said, "It's no use, she's gone."

Michael held out his hand and helped her stand. "Never give up hope," he said.

We kept looking. Another scream echoed through the woods. We ran towards it. When we found Aria she was shaking and standing over a body. It was Jeremiah, his lifeless eyes stared straight forward as if looking right through us. There was blood pooling around his head.

I put my hand on her arm and she collapsed into me. We fell to the ground and I just held her as we cried.

"I only turned my back on him for a minute," she managed to say. "I thought I heard something and when I turned around he was dead."

"What is happening here?" I asked.

"It has to be him." Ava said.

"Who?"

"Daniel Davison."

"That was just a story Jeremiah told to scare us," Michael said. "There never was a Daniel Davison, it was completely made up."

"Then who killed Jeremiah?"

Michael didn't have an answer for that. We all stood there in shocked silence.

"What do we do now?" Aria finally asked. It was the first time I had ever seen her without a plan.

"We keep looking for Audrey." I answered.

"I'm doing what we should have done a long time ago," Michael said. "Calling the police."

He pulled out his phone, "It's dead, hand me one of your phones."

I checked mine, it was dead too. Strange since I had just charged it in the car. Aria and Ava's phones were dead too.

We took a deep breath and started searching again. Michael wanted all of us to stay together, but Ava insisted on two groups, wanting to find Audrey as soon as possible.

As Michael and I walked through the woods I spoke up, "Please say something, if this silence lasts any longer, I swear I'm going to go crazy."

Michael paused before saying, "I guess this is as a good of a time as any, seeing as I'm not sure I will get another chance. As you know we have been friends for our entire lives, and I don't think I am the only one who has noticed that it is starting to become something more. It's no secret that I love you more than anyone I have ever met, and I know that you love me, too. So," he took my hand and got down on one knee, "Emily Nicole Rosewood, if we live through this will you marry me?"

I started crying again, "Of course I will." I kissed him, then took a deep breath as I was reminded of reality, "We should keep looking."

As we began walking we heard Aria scream again. This time it was faint and far away. Michael took my hand so we wouldn't get separated and we ran. When we once again reached the clearing we saw a man digging a hole and four dead bodies on the ground next to him. I sank to the ground and was paralyzed with grief. Michael, however was moved to action with anger. He ran at the stranger from behind and knocked him into the hole. He picked up the shovel and hit him over the head with it until the man stopped struggling. Then he came back to me and held me. We cried together until the cops came.

They identified the man as Daniel Davison, a man who they had been looking for over thirty years for countless murders.

Michael and I survived, that much is true. But I'm not sure you can say we really lived. How can you live after experiencing something like that? It takes away part of who you are and you can never get it back. How can you go on to live a happy life when your friends had theirs stolen away in such a violent manner?

When the Circus Comes to Town

One bright sunny day Lila Brooks took her three small children to see a traveling circus for an afternoon of carefree fun and laughter. The children were in awe as they stepped up to the giant red and white tent with loud music coming from inside. They stopped in front of it, looking up with their eyes wide and mouths open.

Lila smiled and encouraged them to go inside, promising it would only get better. The tent looked much larger on the inside and was full of bright lights, people, and laughter. The performers were everywhere. There was a ringmaster, a fire-eater, an acrobat, a bearded lady, a lion tamer, and plenty of clowns all around.

As Lila and the children took their seats, the grinning ringmaster stepped to the center of the stage. "Welcome," he said brightly. "Welcome one and all! We have a very special show planned for you today. It brings us such joy and delight to see each and every one of you here today. Without further ado, I think it's time we got started!" As he was saying this a dozen clowns ran towards the crowd, pies in hand. The crowd burst out in laughter as the clowns began to shove the pies into the faces of unsuspecting audience members. The laughter stopped suddenly when those who had been hit began to drop to the floor. The acrobat began to throw knives from her high perch on the tightrope, striking audience members with surprising accuracy. The fire-eater set one whole section on fire, people screamed as they tried to get out, but all of the gates were locked. The bearded lady pulled out a dagger and stabbed the people in the front row. The lion tamer released the beast to feed and watched proudly as it attacked the helpless customers. Lila panicked in the chaos as she tried to find an escape for her children. She spotted the sunlight coming through an exit not far from where they sat. She instructed the children to be quiet and to follow her as quickly as they could. She breathed a sigh of relief as they exited the tent and stepped out into the sunlight. As she turned to run she walked into someone. Heart beating fast, she slowly looked up to see the cold, pale blue eyes of the ringmaster.

"Where are you going?" he asked with a smirk. "The fun has only begun."

Willow Hill

There once was a castle called Willow Hill that was set in the English countryside miles away from sight. A grand wedding was planned for Ms. Nancy Hollings and Mr. Edward Clifton. The date was set for a Sunday in April and the wedding party came the Friday before.

Willow Hill was owned by the cousins of the Hollings, Sir Richard and Lady Evelyn Remington, and their mute child, Harrison.

The wedding party began to arrive. The first to appear were, Hugh, the father of the bride, a kind fellow who only wanted the best for his spoiled daughter; Nancy, the conceited bride-to-be, whose condescending smile and empty eyes let you know exactly what she thought of you; Sarah Briezden, a dear friend of the bride, who always had an air of confusion about her; Emma Reel, the bride's best friend: she was an elegant manipulator and a fantastic enemy.

Then Charlotte, Nancy's cousin, who was soft-spoken, yet deeply tormented beneath her mesmerizing blue eyes. Next, in a carriage of her own, came Helen Hollings, the great aunt of the bride-to-be, a regal woman, proud of her social status and breeding. Now being of great age, she could no longer trust her deceitful eyes. She was very loving towards Nancy yet always guarded with Charlotte.

The final arrivals came: Zachary Hayes, the photographer, and a dear friend of the Clifton family; Thomas Bloodworth, the groom's best friend, an arrogant, judgmental young man who believed that his family name could get him whatever he wanted; and finally, Edward, the groom, a compassionate, dapper fellow, who was an independent thinker. He saw how others forced Nancy to live on a pedestal and knew that, with him, she could be free.

The master of Willow Hill, Sir Richard Remington, was a man not clouded by his wealth, he was more than happy to lend the use of his home for his cousin's wedding; his wife, Lady Evelyn was a gentle woman who looked at everyone with kind eyes.

Harrison Remington, at age eight was a simple, free-hearted child who loved to wander around the castle that was his home and was always discovering new passages.

The castle was staffed by the good cook, Phillip Boyer, and his young daughter, Louise, who served as the maid. He was happy with their good fortune, while his daughter was not content.

Then there was Gilbert White, the groundskeeper, he was a loyal employee who viewed the Remingtons as his own family.

Now our story begins. The Remingtons and their guests were in the Dining Hall, when Emma suggested to Nancy that she tell the story of when she and Charlotte were invited to a ball; Charlotte spent hours helping Nancy get ready, only to find that Nancy only had one invitation and had accepted it herself, leaving Charlotte alone at home, waiting to hear of the dance when Nancy returned.

Richard changed the subject by announcing how happy he was for his dear sweet cousin, Nancy.

Evelyn spoke in a soft voice, asking, "When will your parents be joining us, Edward?"

"Unfortunately, my Mother is under the weather. My family will not be joining us until just in time for the ceremony."

Then dessert was served and one by one each guest retired for the night. Charlotte went off to the library to read and be alone; and Sarah joined her.

Charlotte settled down with her favorite little blue book of poems and Sarah began watching the fire. A short moment later she spoke, "Oh! There you are with that little blue book again. My Mother always said, 'Boys like pretty girls, not smart girls.' That is why you will never find me reading, unless it is a small book, with a lot of pictures."

Charlotte rolled her eyes and said, "Well, some girls are pretty... and some are smart." Turning to face Sarah she added, "And some are neither very intelligent nor beautiful."

"Oh Charlotte, you mustn't insult yourself... you are smart enough."

They then sat in silence for a few short moments before Sarah spoke again, "I am happy for Nancy, but I wish Edward would find someone more deserving." She smiled at Charlotte, "Someone kind, graceful, and thoughtful... Well, someone more like me."

Charlotte stood and walked over to the fire to adjust the wood as Sarah continued, "Someone beautiful who would make him happy."

"You are right, he does deserve better." Charlotte answered in a soft voice.

"How could you say something like that?" Sarah asked, shocked. "He is engaged to your cousin!"

As the wind started to howl and thunder boomed, Charlotte took a few steps towards Sarah and lodged the fireplace poker through her neck. The blood gushed out and splattered onto the book that Charlotte still clung to.

She then blew out the candles and retired to her room, hid her bloodstained dress under the bed, and continued reading.

The next morning the house awoke to a scream; it was Lady Evelyn. All rushed to the library to see what it was that had disturbed her. There, to the horror of the guests, was the body. Nancy turned to Emma, crying, and said,

"Now what am I going to do? Sarah was supposed to be one of my bridesmaids," she wiped away a tear before continuing. "I suppose Charlotte could do it..."

"Thank you, cousin," Charlotte replied quietly, staring at the body as if she were in shock.

Richard grabbed the phone in haste to call the police, only to find that the line was dead.

Thomas and Zachary rushed to the carriage. As they descended down the hill they discovered that the estate was surrounded by water. The storm had caused flooding so deep that there was no chance of leaving. Willow Hill was now an island lost to all mankind.

The thirteen remaining occupants of the castle met in the Dining Hall to discuss the events of the previous night.

"Everyone must remain in groups of three or more," Richard said, "Because of the storm, no one could have come to Willow Hill or left last night. The murderer must be among us."

"Dear cousin," Charlotte spoke, "There may have been someone hiding on the estate for days now, waiting for the storm, and knowing that the wedding party would be stuck, as Willow Hill always floods this time of year."

"That is a great possibility, Richard," Evelyn said. "Perhaps Charlotte is right."

Richard, Hugh, Thomas, and Edward searched the grounds, while Phillip and Zachary kept company with the women, and young Harrison played in the corner of the room. Since no one was found hiding on the grounds or the ancient tower at the peak of the estate they moved the search inside the castle.

When their search found nothing, Helen, who had been considered eccentric for years now, said, "Perhaps they came here only to kill Sarah. They may have had a boat and escaped last night before any of us awoke. Let's go to the garden and play croquet."

"Maybe the fresh air would do us all some good." Hugh agreed.

They asked Gilbert if he would take the body to what was to be Sarah's room for the weekend. He placed her on the bed and laid a blanket over her. Then he left her in peace.

After all except Louise and Phillip left, Phillip told her that he would begin to prepare lunch and she was to make the beds.

In Charlotte's room, Louise stood in front of the vanity and looked through her jewelry box. She picked up the blood-stained poetry book and turned, petrified, a look of helplessness painted her eyes. There stood Charlotte, with an antique letter opener she had taken from the dresser. In a hushed tone she said, "That is mine." and she plunged the letter opener into Louise's shoulder. She swiftly stabbed her in the stomach, heart, and face, time and time again; for a total of nineteen times.

Charlotte stood there as her bloody victim fell forward and slid down her. She then threw the letter opener towards the corpse and left the room.

She walked down to the kitchen; Phillip had his back turned and was basting the roast. She grabbed the cleaver from the counter, walked over behind him and said, "I am sorry." Just as he was about to turn she drove the cleaver into the side of his neck, and let out a scream of terror. When everyone else returned she told them with a shaking voice, "I went up to my room and found Louise lying on the floor, I tried to help her but it was too late. Then I came down here knowing that Phillip was inside the house too, and I just found him. The murderer never left. He's still at Willow Hill." She collapsed in her Uncle Hugh's arms.

After Charlotte awoke in her room she changed to a fresh dress and gathered the two bloody gowns, knowing that she needed a more permanent place to hide them.

She walked to the far eastern corner of the estate. There she found the groundskeeper digging a small hole to plant a new bush. She dropped the dresses and went to him, saying, "Gilbert, you work too hard, you should take a break."

He tilted his hat and thanked her. He set the shovel down, wiped the sweat from his brow, and before he knew it he was laying on the ground. Charlotte had hit him in the face with the shovel. She looked at him, shovel in hand and said, "Thank you for digging the hole." she hit him repetitively until he stopped moving. She put the dresses in the hole, then looked back down at her victim, and said, "I will need a bigger hole."After filling in the grave she returned to the castle in time for tea.

Once everyone except Zachary and Charlotte had left, he started a conversation. "Could you please help me with something?" he asked.

She smiled softly.

"I was hoping for a position with a store magazine and I need to take photos of various subjects whose style is similar to their merchandise. You are a young lady who is on top of the fashion world. May I please photograph you in the green dress you wore our first night here?"

Charlotte folded her hands and replied, "I would be glad to help. May I see some of your work?"

"Please excuse me while I fetch my portfolio."

As he excited the room she snooped through his satchel and found a few vials of strange white powder and a vial of some sort of ink. She poured the substances into his tea and stirred it. Then she returned to her seat.

Zachary returned and they spent the next hour looking through his portfolio and enjoying their tea. His eye began to twitch and he gasped for air. Charlotte bid him goodbye and in that moment he passed.

Emma entered the room soon after Charlotte left; she saw Zachary and knew he was gone. Through misty eyes she saw something in the carpet, next to the body – it was one of Charlotte's silver earrings that she had always admired. She took the earring, put it in her pocket, and was about to call for help when she glanced out the window and saw Charlotte standing on the hilltop. She decided to confront her.

Charlotte heard a voice, "I have your earring."

She turned, "Emma! Where did you find it?"

"Next to your latest victim."

"Do you mean Zachary or Gilbert? I get so confused."

Emma gasped, "That is what happened to him? People are starting to suspect he is the killer. How many people have you killed this weekend?"

Charlotte pondered this for a moment and then began to list the victims, "First; there was Sarah, she was the easy one; then Poor Louise never should have gone through my things; Phillip, well, he would have soon found out who killed his daughter; Gilbert was in the wrong place at the wrong time - some may say he even dug his own grave; and Zachary was about to get in my way; so that would be six."

"Six?"

While Emma was still trying to understand this, Charlotte said, "And I thought Sarah was the idiot... you are number six." She pushed her down the hill. She tumbled down, smashing her head open on the grand willow.

Helen walked up behind Charlotte, "Oh dear," she said. "That cranky girl fell down the hill..." she paused before asking, "Did you push her?"

"Yes, Aunt Helen," She caressed her aging aunt's face in her hand, quickly snapped her neck and tossed her down the hill. She returned to the castle to find everyone frantic at finding the body of the young photographer. Now was her chance. Weeping uncontrollably, she said, "I found Aunt Helen and Emma dead at the bottom of the hill. I saw Gilbert fleeing; he got into Richard's boat and left the estate."

Hugh took notice of his distraught niece and took her by the hand, "You need fresh air and to leave this terrible place. Let's go fowl hunting like we used to."

Then, out in the field after a few arrows were shot, Charlotte was beaming. She turned to her uncle and said, "I've missed our alone time. You have been so busy with Nancy getting married."

"I love you, Charlotte." he said. "But you need help."

Her radiant smile then turned to a blank expression.

He continued, "I know it's you, Charlotte. You were the one who had tea with Zachary this afternoon, no one can find the groundskeeper - I know you are the true reason Gilbert has gone missing, Aunt Helen is gone, and I know how you feel about Emma. I can't believe you are doing all of this as Nancy was supposed to be married."

"Why does everything have to be about Nancy? I am important too."

"You are not my daughter."

He saw the rage building in her eyes and tried to back away. She took an arrow in her hand and plunged it through his heart. As he fell to the ground she spoke in a soft voice, "I thought I was your little girl too."

He reached for her ankle and she kicked his hand away, saying, "You are not my father."

Charlotte returned to the castle in a false state of shock, "As we were walking, Uncle Hugh, rest his soul, he was sharpening an arrow, when he fell over a root and the arrow pierced through his heart." She managed to tell the others.

Nancy collapsed on the ivory colored fainting couch. Charlotte rushed to her side, "I cannot believe it either."

Edward came to them, "What were his final words?" he asked.

With a small smile, Nancy said, "Oh, dear Charlotte, please tell me he spoke of me, or even had a message for me."

Charlotte took her cousin's hand in her own and said, "His final words were: 'I am truly thankful I was able to raise you as my own.' I am deeply sorry to say that he did not speak of you."

The room was filled with silence, then Evelyn said, "I must get Harrison to bed. It has been a long day and we could all use some rest."

As the sun rose on what was to be the wedding day, Edward and Nancy announced that they would see if the water had receded. Thomas and Charlotte sat in the parlor and she watched out the window as they drove out of sight.

"Too bad this weekend did not go as planned," Thomas said. "Edward and Nancy deserve better."

She turned to him, her hand resting on the head of an ancient Greek statue. "Nancy always had things easy; it's about time something didn't work out for her." She twisted her hand and snapped the porcelain head from the statue.

In a concerned tone he said, "I should check on Richard and Evelyn. We have not seen them this morning."

Charlotte walked over to him. With an artificial smile and murder beneath her eyes, she told him, "There is no need to worry about them. I slit their throats last night as they slept. Don't pay them any attention." She grabbed his tie, pulling it tighter and tighter and they struggled, until finally, with his last breath he asked for mercy.

She straightened his tie, seated him comfortably, moved the hair from his eyes, and said, "Thomas, it is a shame you were so conceited and ignorant. It should have been you and Nancy together."

When Edward and Nancy returned they found Charlotte sitting on the parlor floor, weeping. Edward rushed to Charlotte's side, took her in his arms, and asked, "What happened?"

Wiping the tears from her eyes, and barely able to speak, she answered, "I went to make tea soon after you left, I came in to find Thomas being strangled... it was some man... I've never seen him before... I was too afraid to stop him. I ran to the kitchen to see him enter the abandoned tower." Edward declared he would follow the killer, leaving for the ruins at once.

As Nancy awaited Edward's return, she began thinking. She turned to Charlotte and said, "Cousin, I haven't heard the kettle yet."

"The kettle...what about the kettle?"

Nancy inched towards the doorway, "If you started the tea as Thomas was being murdered, why isn't it done yet?"

Charlotte pulled her pearl-handled pistol from her skirt pocket, "Nancy," she said in a dry voice, "Do you want me to shoot you now, or would you like to try to run?"

Taking a quick breath, Nancy fled, knowing that Charlotte followed her closely. She ran to the room her father had been staying in, where she knew his rifle was kept. She pointed the gun at Charlotte and said, "Don't do this."

"Go ahead, Nancy, if you think you can shoot me; shoot me."

Nancy, with a shaking hand, pulled the trigger. Nothing happened.

"I can't believe you were actually going to shoot me! It is a good thing I hid your father's bullets after the hunting accident." Charlotte pulled the trigger, shooting Nancy in the chest. "I hope the bullet found your heart, I never could." Nancy fell to the floor.

At the end of the staircase there was a window, Charlotte took a lighter and set the drapes on fire. "So many memories," she said softly.

She rushed to the tower to embrace her beloved. Edward saw her standing there with a gun in her hand and the castle in flames and asked, "Where is Nancy, Charlotte?"

She smiled and said, "Don't worry, Edward. I took care of Nancy; she is no longer in our way."

He slowly retreated back to the tower. As he walked up the stairs Charlotte told a story.

"Remember, Edward? It was so many summers ago, but it feels like just yesterday in my heart. Your family came to stay at my uncle's for the summer. I was thirteen and I was already living there, and Nancy and her friends were being mean to me like always. Don't you remember? Emma came up to me and took my book and tore out all of the pages. You wiped my tears, and after dinner that night you gave me your book of poetry. I still have that little blue book. It's in my pocket, it is the only thing I couldn't bear to see go up in flames. And then you went away from my life, but I know you kept me in your heart as I kept you in mine. I don't know what happened, but now it is five years later and you were engaged to marry Nancy. I couldn't understand it. She must have tricked you in some way. She lied to you. Made you think she was kind, but I took care of the liar. And on this, what was going to be the day of your biggest mistake, you can marry me, and from this day on all our dreams can come true."

Edward spoke, "I remember that day, but after I gave you that book, I remember something else. You took a candle and lit Emma's hair on fire. Hugh had you put away for four years. We all thought you were better now. I can't believe you did the things you did, after your Uncle Hugh took you in, he couldn't believe that you set that fire at your home when you were only eleven - the fire that killed your parents and your brothers and sisters."

Before Edward could go on, Charlotte started to pull her hair and screamed "Lies!"

Now at the top of the tower, he felt the cold air blowing across the sky. He said "Charlotte, you need to understand this, I loved Nancy. She was the love of my life. You killed her - you crushed my heart and killed my soul - you took everything from me. You're crazy, I've never loved you and I never could."

"You don't mean that, Edward, do you?"

"Of course I do, you are a demon, and an evil, wicked woman."

"Fine!" Charlotte screeched as she shot out another bullet. Edward fell to the ground and was gone.

As Charlotte looked down at what she had done she heard a faint voice calling in the distance. She began her search. As she walked down the old hill she saw Nancy rushing to find Edward. Her dress was bloodstained, her hair was singed, and she struggled for every breath.

"Nancy!" Charlotte exclaimed with a grin, "Look at you! I guess I am the pretty one now."

Nancy screamed, "Edward!" Still trying to find her love.

"Oh, Edward is gone." Charlotte said.

Nancy, nearly stumbling over her dress, attempted to run down the hill. In her state, Charlotte could keep up just by walking. As she reached the edge of the estate she found that the water was still too deep to escape, and turned to face her cousin. She took a breath and said, "Charlotte, just shoot me!"

"I suppose that would be the humane way," Charlotte said. She aimed her gun for the sky, shot off four bullets and said, "Unfortunately I am out of ammo." She tossed her gun to the side as Nancy fell to her knees and asked, "Are you just going to let me bleed to death?"

Charlotte walked to her cousin and placed her hands on her shoulders, "I won't let you bleed to death, I don't want to hear you complain." she pushed Nancy down, forcing her into the water, she sat on her stomach as she held her cousin down. Nancy struggled at first, but the fight was soon over.

Once Nancy was dead Charlotte rolled her body into the water. She stood there for a moment watching her cousin drift. Then she screamed to the sky, "I can still be with Edward!" She ran up the hill and into the tower and looked at her beloved's corpse, "I'm coming to join you, Edward!" she screamed and then she jumped. Charlotte hit her head on a large rock at the bottom, splitting it open.

Immediately the sun moved from behind the clouds and the flood waters started to recede. The police found Harrison two days later sleeping under the cherry trees.

Miss Wishard

Miss Wishard was a young teacher who took her work very seriously. So in 1942 when she got her first set of students, she promised they would learn one good lesson.

Her class was small, only ten children. The room was rather small and stuffy; she opened all the windows and put flowers in a vase on her desk, on the chalkboard she wrote "Miss Wishard." The children started to enter the room and attendance was taken. "All right, let's get to work!" She said with a smile. She turned to the board and heard ten books drop. She looked to the students, "Pick up the books!" She said dryly with her fist tight. She resumed to writing on the board. Then all the students coughed and started to laugh when she looked back to them, she went on with the lesson and tried her best to keep calm.

After the bell rang all the children gathered their things, and before they left Miss Wishard gave them all a first day treat, cookies and lemonade. Oh, how the children devoured them, not one crumb or chocolate chip was left. All the lemonade was gone, those glasses were left dry. Miss Wishard watched as all the little children started to faint. "Bless their hearts" she said as she gathered her pencils and rat poison from her desk. All the little children were found that night and buried within the week. Miss Wishard was never heard from again.

Hitchhiker

"Thank you, Mark! Thank you so much for taking us to the concert!" Jessica squealed as they started the long trip home.

"Well, it is your birthday after all." Mark replied, "and you're the only little sister I have."

Along with them were their cousin Zach, and her best friends Gina and Stephanie.

"Let's put the CD in now!" Gina suggested.

Soon music was blaring from the car.

Jessica turned the music down after a while and asked, "What's that?"

In the headlights they saw something at the side of the road. As they came closer, Mark slowed down to look. There was man trying to get a ride.

"Should we stop?" Stephanie asked, "Maybe he needs help."

"No," Mark replied as he returned to the speed limit. "You can't trust anyone anymore. I'm sure he will get help some other way, but my job is to make sure you all get home safely."

"I hope he'll be okay," Gina said. "I understand why we can't stop, but I just have a bad feeling about this."

"Come on, Gina." Zach said, "you're not Mother Teresa. Let's just move on."

Jessica turned the music up again only for Mark to turn it off when they heard clinking. The noise soon stopped and they continued in silence until they heard a loud squealing.

Mark pulled to the side of the road. "I think that's the brakes. We aren't far from home now, I'll call someone to come get us." He checked his phone, "We're still too far from the city, does anyone have a signal?"

They all checked their phones but they were too far out of range. It was still too far to walk home so Mark told them to stay in the car as he tried to find a signal.

As Mark walked out of sight Zach laughed, "What a great way to end your birthday, Jess, stranded in the middle of nowhere."

"A little adventure never hurt anyone," Jessica replied. "Maybe we'll get a good story out of it."

"I'd like to get home before school starts tomorrow." Stephanie said.

Jessica laughed, "That's true, I hope Mark can reach someone."

Gina shivered, "It's getting really cold, did Mark take the keys with him?"

Jessica checked the car, "I guess he did, I don't see them here."

"I'm going to go get them, who knows how long he will be gone."

As she opened the car door Zach spoke up, "You should stay in the car, it will be colder outside. Besides," he grinned. "who knows what could be lurking out there."

"That's not funny!" Stephanie exclaimed. "Be careful. And find out if Mark has been able to contact anyone."

"Yes, ma'am." he replied, tipping an imaginary hat.

"He thinks he's *so* funny," Stephanie said, rolling her eyes and blushing a little.

"You have got to be kidding me," Jessica said, staring at her friend in disbelief.

"What are you talking about?"

"Please tell me you don't like my cousin."

"Zach?" Stephanie asked, feigning shock. "Where would you get that idea? He's annoying and weird and I'm pretty sure a little crazy."

"You do like him!" Gina exclaimed.

"Shh," Stephanie whispered. "He might be close enough to hear."

"Sorry," Gina said, fighting laughter. "I'm just so happy for you."

"Happy for me? What do you mean?"

"You two are going to get married."

"Okay, maybe I misspoke earlier," Stephanie said, "obviously you're the crazy one."

"You know it's true. Who would have thought? Stephanie and Zach. I have to admit, you guys would be pretty adorable."

"Can we change the subject? He doesn't even like me like that."

"Of course he does, Steph. How could he not?"

"Leave her alone," Jessica said. "I'm sorry, Steph, I didn't realize that you actually cared about him."

"It's fine, let's just talk about something else." she paused. "Mark's been gone for a while, hasn't he?"

Gina checked her phone, 2:45 am. She sighed, "I am so gonna fail that English test tomorrow."

"I'm serious," Stephanie said. "I'm worried about them. I'm going to go look."

"Are you sure that's a good idea?" Jessica asked, fear evident in her voice. "They went on their own and who knows what could have happened to them. Maybe I should go with you."

"What about me?" Gina asked.

"Someone has to stay here in case they come back so you can tell them where we went. Lock all the doors and keep an eye out for anything strange."

As her friends left Gina took a deep breath and tried to be brave. Fifteen minutes later she heard the sound of a twig snapping underneath a heavy boot. She looked up and saw a shadowy figure approaching the car.

The next morning the local police discovered the bodies of five teenagers scattered along a road about 7 miles out of town.

A Perfect Dinner

It was nearly 4:00 in the afternoon, Thanksgiving Day, 1953. Minnie Madison, an angel of a house wife, was preparing to host Thanksgiving dinner for the first time with her husband of five months, Michael, a successful young lawyer who she wanted to make happy.

There was a knock, Minnie, a petite, golden blonde with eyes blue and wide like the sky, donning a white and black polka dot dress answered the door to find her sister-in-law, Marla and her husband, Carl. Marla had dark brown hair and green eyes like her brother; Carl was an auburn-haired man with brown eyes. Minnie's smile soon vanished and she uttered these words, "Oh, look who's here two hours early."

They both shouted, "Surprise!"

"I thought I would help you make dinner." Marla said.

"Come in," Minnie said. "Make yourselves comfortable." They did just that. Minnie continued, "Thank you, but I won't be needing your help, Marla. I want to prove to Michael that I can make the perfect Thanksgiving dinner."

"Where is Mikey?" Carl asked.

"Michael just left," Minnie explained. "he went to get some French vanilla ice cream." With that she returned to the kitchen.

She removed the turkey from the oven to baste it once again. A cold hand was placed on her shoulder. She shrieked, dropping the pan on the floor. Before Marla could say "I'm sorry" Minnie rammed her meat thermometer through her sister-in-law's throat. As she fell to the ground, Minnie looked down, "What luck, none of your blood got on my new dress."

As Minnie put the turkey back into the oven, Carl walked into the kitchen. He knelt beside his departed wife. Minnie stood behind him, "Carl, you never should have come early." Then she hit him in the back of the head with her cast iron skillet. She looked to her cluttered floor and said, "I guess I will have to see if they fit under the bed."

Shortly after the kitchen was once again spotless there was another knock. She opened the door to find an aging couple. She hugged the bald man with glasses covering his brown eyes. With joy, she exclaimed, "Uncle Delphas!" Then she hugged the woman standing next to him whose black curls framed her blue eyes."Aunt Peggy!"

"Where is our nephew?" She asked.

"He is getting French vanilla ice cream and should be back any minute."

Standing behind this couple was their daughter Darlene, a younger version of her mother, with her husband, Fred Porter.

"Come in everyone," Minnie said with a smile. "Dinner is on its way."

She returned to the kitchen to start the stuffing and Peggy followed. Minnie turned around when she heard glass shattering. There stood Peggy with a broken cup at her feet. "I'm sorry," She said.

Minnie picked up her cast iron skillet once again as her aunt bent over to pick up the pieces. "You should be sorry." She said. "I promised Michael a perfect Thanksgiving dinner. And other than my skillet, that glass was the only thing I had left that belonged to my mother." She began to bash her head in. Aunt Peggy lied there, lifeless, on the floor. She took her outside to the back porch and covered her with garbage bags.

She came back into the kitchen to find Darlene stirring her cranberry sauce. She slammed the door behind her, and with a nervous chuckle she asked, "What do you think you are doing?"

Darlene removed the spoon and set it on top of the open cookbook. She looked at Minnie with questioning eyes, "Where's my mother?" she asked.

"She stepped out for air."

"Why isn't Marla here yet?"

"Marla and Carl are running late and if all they get is macaroni and cheese, then too bad." Minnie grabbed her marble rolling pin, "Darlene, did you love your grandmother?"

"Yes, of course."

"Do you have anything that belonged to her?"

"I have her silk tablecloth."

"How would you feel if someone stained it with cranberry sauce?" She asked with her teeth clenched.

"Well, I think I'd be mad enough I could kill someone." She laughed.

"Me too," Minnie laughed. She quickly crammed a dish towel into Darlene's mouth. She began to beat her with the marble rolling pin, enjoying the sound of each bone cracking. Darlene's struggle was soon over. Minnie conveniently stored her in the closet with the mop and broom.

Minnie walked into the living room to find Delphas standing at her glass-topped wet bar that now had a large crack through it.

"Oh Minnie, I dropped the cocktail shaker and it cracked the top, and when I went to get it I sliced my hand on the broken glass. Now there is blood all over my sleeve."

"Alright, Uncle Delphas, just come into the bathroom and I'll take care of you."

Now at the sink she dabbed his blood stain with a wet cloth.

"Minnie, what is taking Peggy and Darlene so long in the kitchen?"

With a sweet smile she said, "Uncle Delphis, your wife and your daughter both tried to ruin my perfect dinner, they had to pay the price."She reached for Michael's straight-blade razor and rammed it though his ear before he could respond to what she had said.

"Okay, Uncle Delphis it's time to get in the tub so you don't bother Michael's boss, Mr. McCray or his wife. This has to be the perfect dinner."

After she got him into the tub and as she closed the curtain she asks "Now, where is Michael with that French vanilla ice cream?"

As she made her way down the hall to the living room she finds Fred whose tie needed fixed. "Let me straighten your tie."

"Alright, thanks Minnie." He smiled at her "I bet this is going to be a real nice dinner."

Her eyes looked empty as she started to pull on his tie, making it tighter and tighter, he was now on his knees gasping for air. "I'm sorry Fred, but I can't have an uneven amount of people at my table. This is going to be a perfect dinner." Then it was over.

She put his body in the coat closet, now hoping all her corpses would stay put until after dinner. She made her way back to the kitchen for the turkey's final basting and rest of the finishing touches. Dinner was now ready to be served, and then there was a loud knock at the door. "That must be Mr. and Mrs. McCray" she said with an almost singing fashion.

She let in a well-to-do couple dressed in fine clothes; taking his hat she saw his black hair that was slowing turning grey, and his wife's fox coat, that nearly matched

her red hair. She placed them in the coat closet and smiled at Fred.
Mr.McCray asked, "Where is Mike?

"Michael went to the market to get us some French vanilla ice cream, so this will be a perfect dinner. Please be seated."

Then Mrs. McCray asked, "Minnie, who are these other chairs for?'

"Michael's family, sadly they all must be under the weather. "

Mrs. McCray once again spoke "Are you sure you want us to start without Michael?'

"Yes, Mrs. McCray, Michael knew what time dinner was to be served, so if all he gets is macaroni and cheese that is all his fault."

After a few bites Mr. McCray said "Minnie, I'll need salt if you want me to eat this turkey."

She stood, "I'll get the shaker from the kitchen." She smiled repeating under her breath "This was supposed to be a perfect dinner."
Minnie returned with the salt shaker in her hand and a cleaver behind her back. She stood behind Mr. McCray's chair putting the shaker in front of him, then plunging the cleaver in to his back and removing it with ease.

"I do love your table cl..." Mrs. McCray began, she stopped as she saw her husband fall into his plate. She screamed, "Ira, My Ira!"

With one spiteful swipe of the blade she beheaded Mrs.McCray "It is so impolite to yell at the dinner table. "

Now, in the kitchen once again, she was ready to serve pie, when Michael finally walked though the backdoor.

"Minnie, I'm so sorry. I had to go to three different stores and the traffic was unbearable. But I finally found the ice cream you wanted. Nothing is too good for my little perfectionist." He then kissed her on the cheek

"Alright, alright go say hello to everyone while I serve dessert"

Michael entered the living room and was overwhelmed by what he saw. In the chair closest to him was his sister Marla, with a large bloody hole in her throat. Next to her was her husband Carl whose head was caved in, then Aunt Peggy with more severe wounds, then Uncle Delphis with the straight blade still sticking out of his head. Then Darlene, who was covered in welts, then Fred whose face was frozen with terror, then his boss Mr. McCray, laying face down on the table, next to him was a headless woman, he walked around the table to see Mrs. McCray's lifeless eyes looking up at him.

Then the kitchen door flung open, there stood Minnie, enraged, holding a pint of ice cream she screamed, "I told you and I told you, I need French vanilla, not plain vanilla. Why is everyone trying to ruin my perfect dinner?"

She threw the ice cream at Michael, and then made her way to her sewing box, retrieving her foot long scissors. He ran for the door, and unknown to him it was locked. Those few moments turned out to be crucial, he felt the blades enter his back. He slid to the ground. As he took his last breath, his loving wife whispered softly, "Let's have pie."

As Minnie Madison enjoyed her perfect dinner full of friends and loved ones she soon realized something and started to laugh. "Silly me," she said, "I forgot the rolls."

The House on Opal Road

The sound of children's laughter could be heard and the smell of cotton candy and corn dogs filled the air. The autumn sky was brightened by many carnival lights. Anna, a young woman new to this town found great joy in this travelling fair. She soon found herself in front of a gypsy's tent. An older woman, wrinkled and gray, exited, "Such a beautiful, fair girl with phoenix feather red hair must have a bright future ahead." she told her, "Come let Lola tell you your future." She led her into the paisley colored tent. She sat her down at a small, round table. "Now, tell me your name, dear."

The young woman replied, "It's Anna."

The gypsy shouted, "Oh, yes, yes, I had a feeling it might be! How would you like Madame Lola to tell you your future? I have a mystical deck of tarot cards from the west, I can read you tea leaves from China, or we can glimpse into your future through a crystal ball I received from a prince I once knew. Make your choice and I will tell you your fate."

"Let's just use the crystal ball." Anna suggested.

Lola ran her hands over the ball over and over again, "Ah, now I see something!" she exclaimed. "You're new here, you haven't any friends. You will meet someone tonight who will play a vital role in your life." Terror filled Lola eyes as she continued, "I see nothing more, I tell you. Now go home and rest. Stay safe."

Anna, disturbed by the gypsy's reaction, left five dollars on the table and exited the tent. On her way out she bumped into a man with light blonde hair and intense green eyes. She felt pulled to him in a way. Yet she wanted to return home. She said, "I'm sorry."

"You shouldn't be sorry," he answered, "this isn't your fault at all."

She left the fairgrounds and all of its wonder, making her way on the town's old, brick sidewalks. Six blocks later she reached Opal Road, returning to her unfamiliar home. It was a white painted Victorian home full of old world charm, enclosed by a black cast iron fence.

She opened the red door to the cold emptiness of her new living room. There was not much there except for old furniture left by the most recent owner and many boxes. As she walked across the room she flinched, still not used to the floors creaking. She went into the kitchen and filled her kettle with water for tea. She was drawn away from the stove by a knock at the door. When she looked out at the porch there no was one there. She told herself it must just be a prank from a neighborhood kid.

She took a seat on the dusty old couch and began to unpack a box of books which she then put on a shelf. As she put the last one in place there was another knock. She looked out the window and once again saw an empty porch. She then nearly leaped out of her skin as the forgotten kettle whistled. Once she poured herself a steaming cup of tea she returned to the living room. She found the books she had just placed on the shelf stacked neatly on the coffee table. She dropped her tea cup and it shattered into a million pieces. She told herself, "I must be exhausted, books don't move on their own."

She realized that she forgot to pack her broom and not seeing one in the hall closet she then thought to look in the basement. After searching for a short time she found it. She came to the bottom of the stairs and saw that the door was now closed. She set down the broom and tried to open the door with no success. So she went back down to look for a crowbar. When she found one and reached the stairs again she saw the door wide open.

She came up the stairs with the broom in one hand and the crowbar in the other. Then after checking all of the doors and windows she searched the house and found nothing out of place. Finally returning once more to the living room she found the broken remains of the tea cup had vanished. Once again she believed it must be her tired mind playing tricks and decided she should go to sleep. She was only asleep for a moment or two before she was awoken by the screaming of her fire alarm. Not finding any smoke or sign of a flame she blamed it on old wiring and reset the alarm. As she made her way up the stairs there was yet another knock. She once more looked out the window to find no one was there. She turned out the lights and prayed that all would be fine.

She slowly walked upstairs, trying not to be frightened too much by the creaking under her feet. She made her way down the long hallway and into her bedroom. Once she had stepped through the doorway she bolted for the safety of her bed. As she laid there she started to drift to sleep and she felt someone pull her blanket from the foot of the bed. With fear in her heart she pulled back. She waited in terror as a minute passed, then screamed as a large, gloved hand came from under her bed and grabbed her arm.

The Calloway County Murders

In the summer of 1979 a small farming town in Kentucky was baffled by an unexplained string of murders.

The first occurred on the night of June 23rd. James Blackthorn was at home working late in his office when he heard a noise coming from the kitchen. He assumed that his wife must have dropped something and since he heard nothing else he returned to his files. He heard a door slam shut and this time went to see what was going on.

Cheryl Blackthorn was lying on the kitchen floor in a pool of her own blood. There was a large knife plunged into her stomach. Unable to move or speak, he stood in the doorway in shock. A few minutes later he was able to call the police and the investigation began. There were no fingerprints, and James could think of no one with a motive for murder.

The following week an even greater tragedy occurred. A nine year old girl's throat had been slit open. Kelly Johnson was found lying on the sidewalk in front of her house. The police found two connections between the murders: there was no evidence at either scene and they were the only murders to occur in ten years.

Tension began to build as the town wondered if there may be a serial killer among them. The only link between Cheryl and Kelly was that Mrs. Blackthorn taught 3rd grade history at Kelly's school.

The final killing happened on July 12th. Evelyn Thomas was found in her living room, having been stabbed six times. When the police arrived they found her nine year old son, Denny, sitting on the couch, staring blankly at his mother. When asked what happened to her, he calmly replied, "I stabbed her with the scissors because she went on a date while Father was away."

"Why would you do that?" Officer Bright asked in shock. "Mama said that people who do bad things deserve to be punished." he said simply.

After Denny confessed to all three murders he was committed to the Calloway County Insane Asylum, where his father was already a patient.

The Beast of Hazel Lake

"The year was 1861, when Uma, a powerful and fierce witch found out that her husband was untrue. So she cursed the young milkmaid named Priscilla who was found in his arms to live out the rest of her days as a beast. Her beauty would wither away and she would forever be in solitude; over time she grew bitter and soon turned violent and bloodthirsty. The townspeople lived in fear of this beast. Unknown to the people of Hazel Lake an inhuman baby was soon born. Because of this, all of her future descendants would also be cursed. Even now, hundreds of years later, there are rumors that the beast still walks the forest."

Three screams echoed through the woods. The Raddford children's Mother had come up behind them and touched the arms of the two boys. The Father laughed, "Okay, time for bed."

"Great, now that you scared us we can go to sleep," The girl said.

"Odella, don't fear, be the one who is feared." The mother said.

After the children went to sleep all cozy in their sleeping bags, The mother and father sat by the fire enjoying the last few embers.

"Holly, I know this must be hard, visiting Hazel Lake without stopping by to see your mother, she was a great lady"

"Thanks, David." She said with a kiss on his cheek. "But you know, being here in the woods where we spent our summers is just what I needed. In fact I know mother is watching."

"That's a nice thought," David commented. "Yes, I'm sure she is."

They sat there together enjoying the silence until the fire had completely burnt out.

The next couple of days went well, with fishing, hiking, and swimming in the nearby lake from which the town got its name. Then, on the night before the last day of the trip David went to get firewood and didn't return.

After about a half hour the family began to worry.

"Why hasn't Dad come back yet?" the youngest son asked. "I'm not sure, Riley." his mother answered. "But I'm sure everything is fine. He will be back before you know it." And so they waited. An hour passed.

"Mom, I'm really worried." Odella said.

"There is nothing to worry about honey; I will go see what is going on." She looked to the oldest of her children, "Paul, I need you to watch out for animals and keep your siblings safe."

Not much was said as the kids sat alone at the campground. Each was scared, but unwilling to state their fears out loud.

After an hour their mother returned, her eyes flooded with tears. "I'm sorry children; I can't find your Father anywhere. He has the keys and without him I don't know what we're going to do."

With false confidence, Paul put his arms around his Mother and said, "We'll find Dad, don't worry." "Maybe we should try splitting up."

"Mom, you and Riley stay together, I can go with Paul." Odella suggested.

"No, you stay with me Odella."

"But don't you think Riley would be safer with you?" Paul asked.

His Mother pulled him aside, "I don't want Riley to see me this upset." she explained.

"Okay, I understand." He said.

They walked as the sun began to set and sent streams of light through the trees. Odella gasped as they came across a disturbing sight. There was a pile of bones a few feet away from them. She was brought to tears as she looked over and saw the bloody, half eaten carcasses of her Father and two brothers. She fell to the ground, kicking and screaming in vain. Then she heard her Mother's stern voice.

"Odella, get off the ground."

She looked up and saw that the tears were gone from her Mother's eyes, "Did you have something to do with this?" She asked.

Before Holly could reply there was a menacing growl from behind her.

Odella screamed and tried to find her footing. There was a creature much like a lion, covered in gray fur, with soulless, piercing, red- glowing eyes, and enormous black claws dripping in blood. She cringed as she felt the steam- like breath on her face.

"Don't worry, Odella, this is why I brought you here." Her mother said, "This is your destiny. The legend is true. Your Grandmother didn't actually die two years ago; she is fulfilling her part of our story."

She took Odella's hand and lifted her up, pushed her hair behind her ears, and said, "You are one of the elite, a daughter of Priscilla. This is our curse and our blessing. My Mother is truly going to leave this earth soon, and it will be my honor to be the beast of Hazel Lake. In a few years, you must start a family and have a daughter, show her the ways, and bring me your sons as tribute. It may seem harsh but you must honor your Mother."

Odella looked at the beast, now knowing that it was her Grandmother, and strangely found pride and comfort in that knowledge.

Watchful Eyes

Part One: Stalker

It was a dark, cloudy night. It was as if the stars had abandoned the sky. Only the moon illuminated the cornfield nearby. There sat a car, unable to run. Red lights blinked as the windows started to fog. I made my way down the cracked blacktop road. My heart started to pound as I closed in. There she sat in the driver's side, she was the most beautiful girl I ever saw. It took me four long, agonizing years to track her down again. I softly knocked on her window, "Veronica, why have you been hiding from me?" She screamed. She was swift; soon she was out the passenger door. And once again the chase was on.

We were in the cornfield. I could hear her breathing heavily as she pushed the stalks out of her way. I ran after her, seeing her fiery red hair swaying in front of me. She was like a matador teasing the bull. She started to scream for help, yet no one would come to her rescue. She would turn right, I would follow; she would turn left, I was right behind her. I warned her, "Veronica, you are only making me angry." I could tell she was getting weaker. She was beginning to stumble, I then started to slow down, I wasn't ready for the fun to stop.

She couldn't bear to run any more, finally I had her in my grasp. She let out an ear-piercing shriek and for one short moment I worried that someone might hear. I had to shut her up, we were at the edge of the road, "Hush now, my sweet." I said and rammed her head into the pavement. I held her in my arms like the doll that she was. I looked into her angel-like face and whispered sweet nothings into her ear. After a few slumberous moments had passed her blue eyes opened. "Don't be scared," I told her, "it will all be over soon." I took my ice pick and ran it through her temple. She died in my arms, the way it was meant to be. I then marked her name off of my list.

Part Two: Disturbed

It had been six months since my last dream came to life. I stood in a dark alley looking at the fifth floor of an office building. There it was, the only window still lit at this hour. A short moment passed and before I knew it I was at her office door. I watched her lovingly through the window. Her platinum hair was barely held together in a loose bun. It had been six hours since I saw her outside the coffee shop. Four months ago, I spotted her at a restaurant when they called her name. The stars were aligned and I knew that she would be mine. I watched her. There was silence, beautiful silence. A place where she was so at peace would become my playground. I laid my hand on the glass and slowly opened the door. Cautiously I crept behind her. With each step I worried my beating heart would give me away. Taking a slowly drawn breath I whispered into her perfect ear, "It's your turn."
I saw her shoulders tense and could feel her eyes widen. She ran. I stayed just close enough. I knew her patterns by now. Poor dear, in all this confusion she ran to the elevator and franticly hit the button before she remembered it was out of order. She spun around to see my face once again. Mascara-stained tears ran down her face. Our chase led to the stairway. I heard the clicking of her high heels as she fled down the stairs, it was chased by the squeaking of my boots as I bolted after her. I was the lion and she was the gazelle. On the last step, a sign that the fates were on my side, her heel snapped. I jumped, soaring over the last five steps and landing on the tile floor next to her. Unable to walk, she drug herself across the floor to a corner. I slowly approached her once more, my shadow cast over her. Her green eyes looked up at me as she simply asked, "Why?"

I laughed and answered, "Because you were chosen, Vera."

I crouched down, cupped her face in my hands, and rammed the back of her head into the wall. She was asleep. She looked so peaceful, just like the first night I watched her. I pulled my hammer from my pocket and kissed her forehead, she had served her purpose. Once again I let my rage overcome. Using swift, jagged motions the prongs of my hammer tore at her skin. Her crimson blood splashed onto me like warm water on a spring day. My work now complete, I left her in the corner like a child that was done with their doll. As I began my next journey I crossed her name off of my list

Part Three: Unexpected

My path was once again clear. Yet at a quarter to eight my eyes grew weary. Seeing a roadside truck stop, I pulled over for a break. When I entered the small diner a girl who meant nothing said, "Follow me." and led me to a table in the back. I was only going to be there for a moment until I heard, "My name's Val, can I take your order?"
I looked up to see a pair of dark brown eyes and chestnut curls reaching to her name tag that read, *Valerie*
I said, "Coffee."
She waited a moment before asking, "Is there anything else?"
I handed her the menu and she got the point.
This wasteland was too full, I had to wait until the time was right. I didn't know which was louder, the beating of my heart, or the ticking of the clock.
As Valerie brought the coffee to my table, two old men that were arguing about the weather left.
8:37 - The mother with her two brats finally left.
My focus was interrupted when that useless girl from before saw my empty cup and asked if I wanted a refill. She took my silence as a no.
8:59 - The two teenagers date ended and they left.
Valerie returned to my table, asking if I wanted a refill. I nodded.
9:17 - A middle aged man and his child left.
Both of the waitresses were in the back and I was now alone. I made my way to the counter. Valerie re-entered the room and was shocked to see I had moved. The fear on her face was exciting. Without asking she brought me

another cup of coffee. It's rather funny, she thought she could read my mind.

The insignificant waitress came back, this time carrying her jacket and seeming in a hurry. She said, "I've got a date, Val. Clock out for me at closing time. It's dead here anyways."

"No problem." Valerie answered, tucking her brown curls behind her left ear, her eyes scanning the deserted restaurant.

9:30 - A burly man walked over to Valerie, "I don't think anyone here will need a meal, so I'm going to go home." "Sure thing, once this fellow finishes his coffee I will close up."

As I heard a car drive off I knew my moment had arrived. "I'm going to go in the kitchen and start cleaning, if you decide you want any food I still have the deep fryer going."

I took another sip of my coffee and made my way into the kitchen. She was standing at the chopping block, texting someone with one hand while the other rested on the counter. She didn't even notice me. In mere seconds I grabbed the knife and chopped off her thumb. Her phone hit the floor, blood was everywhere, she screamed in agony. She ran. I waited so long for this part. She was faster than the others. She was cornered. She grabbed a meat fork and pointed it right at me. I laughed, finally one that wanted to play. With my knife still in hand we both tried to get in a few good strikes. As I thrusted forward she stabbed my hand and the knife clattered to the floor. She hit the ground, she had lost too much blood.

Her eyes fluttered open as I held her above the deep fryer. She screamed. She couldn't get free. Her hands were tied together and my body pressed hers to the side. Placing my

hands on her upper back, I pressed down, sinking her into the bubbling oil. She convoluted and then all was still.
I was free to go and able to focus on my list again.

Part Four: Unhinged

I'd waited so long and now I was almost where I needed to be. After this one I would be ready for my grand finale. There it was, like always before, that little yellow house with daisies in the front yard. It was revolting. It looked the same as it had eight years ago; the last time I saw it. She always thought that she was so safe here. She could never imagine that her life would end by my hand, because my life was destroyed by hers.

It was a cloudy afternoon; I walked to the door and peered through the window. I could see the grey curls on top on her head as she sat in her pink chair facing away from me. My anger grew as I heard her shouting the answers at her game show. I saw her disgusting wrinkled hand as she reached for her yarn to knit. Time passed. She stood and made her way to the kitchen, passing a mirror; she gazed at her reflection and must have been hoping for an improvement. After a moment in the kitchen she returned to the living room, how could she have known I was hiding in the closet?

Night fell and I heard the bathroom door creak open. I left the closet and made my way to her hideous pink chair. From the basket I gathered the scissors, some yarn, and the potholder she had just finished. I set a trap. Then I waited beneath her bed.

She tripped over the umbrella that I put in the doorway, and blacked out as she hit her head on the corner of her dresser. I hungered for the look of panic in her eyes. Finally she was awake. She struggled to break the yarn that held her ankles and wrists together. In the dark she screamed, "Help!" I stepped out of the shadows and recognition flooded her face. She stuttered as she tried to speak, "You..." She finally managed before I gagged her with her potholder. I caressed her face. "Normally at this point they ask me why. But you know why, Velma." Tauntingly, I waved her scissors in her face. In a frenzy I started puncturing her full of holes. Her bed was stained with blood and tears. I could feel her still breathing, and as I covered her with her quilt I said, "Sleep well."

I crossed her name off of my list and waited.

Part Five: Finally

I was waiting for hours, desperately needing to see her reaction. At last I heard the front door being unlocked. I knew the time would soon come. I heard her call out, "Mother!" I smiled at the thought that she would never hear an answer. I watched from the louvred closet door as she entered the bedroom and saw the blankets pulled over Velma.

She reached out and put her hand on her mother's arm, "Mother, wake -" she stopped suddenly when she noticed a dark spot spreading across the blanket. She pulled her hand back and started shaking as the saw that it was red. She was still trembling as she pulled the blanket back to see my best work. She sank to the floor, lost for words. She couldn't even scream.

I made my presence known. Her face was painted with fear as she uttered my name. "Joe," she said, "Mother was right, you are crazy."

I replied with a laugh, "You're the one that made me crazy. You left me for Phil, my best friend. After six years you were done with me. Now it's time for you to pay for your sins. Run Victoria."

And she did. She made her way to the living room. I grabbed her by the wrist and pulled her back. I let her escape and she ran to the kitchen. I slowly walked in to find her frantically looking through the drawers. "Victoria, sweetheart, I hid all the knives." I said calmly, then I yelled, "Look what you made me do!" I ripped open my shirt to reveal the V that I had carved into myself.

She pointlessly continued to search for a weapon, her back turned to me. I came behind her, grabbed her hair, and pulled her back. She had the gall to strike my face

with an ice cream scoop. I slammed her face into the
counter top.

I told her, "Because of you dozens of women have died."
She cowered on the floor as blood ran down her china doll
face. I touched her back and said, "You keep making me
do things I hate myself for."

I went to whisper something in her ear, and was taken
back by sharp pain as she rammed her fingers into my
eyes. Like a fool I covered them. When I looked she was
gone. I heard her say, "I need help, I'm at - " I knew she
was on the phone. I bolted for the living room. I jumped
her, her phone fell to the floor. She was struggling to get
away and I was struggling to win. In the background we
heard the 911 operator asking for the address. I pulled out
the gun I had given her years ago. "Remember this?" I
taunted her. "I told you that you would need it."

I had her pinned to the ground. There was a stinging pain
in my side, she had Velma's other pair of scissors. I
dropped the gun and stood to remove the scissors. I was a
fool. I let her escape again. I looked up and she was
holding the gun.

"I guess you were right, Joe. I did need this."
The last thing I knew was a flash of light.

A Chill in the Air: A Collection of Stories and Poetry

Sandlin

Playtime

A Chill in the Air: A Collection of Stories and Poetry

My, Oh My

From freshly picked berries I baked a pie

I served it with milk in case it was dry

With just one taste they would surely die

I smiled when Daddy started to cry

And then when blood came out Mommy's eye

But the neighbor girl ruined it, she had to spy

Now in the cornfield her cold body does lie

If you ask me my story I will tell you why

None of this I can deny

Come on in, have a slice of pie

Bernice's Bullet

I didn't know the gun was loaded

I didn't mean to take their life away

I didn't know the gun was loaded

Now all the other kids are running away! Bang! Bang!

Among the Hanging Clothes

In the bedroom closet, deep in the corner hides a monster

Behind the little children's rod for hanging clothes

A mouth of a hundred sharp, yellow, blood-stained teeth

With long, curled claws spouting from its fingers and toes

It waits for night when parents sleep, then the door will creak

This devilish thing leaps across the room and latches onto you

You are a goner, poor child; you will never again breathe or speak

What a Doll

There she is sitting in her little chair

Blue glass eyes and blonde silky hair

Porcelain skin and cheeks of soft rose

Crimson painted lips and Victorian clothes

Something is wrong with her crooked smile

I know she slowly moves once in a while

I feel she is watching with those piercing bright eyes

Yet when I look at her, completely still she lies

I can hear her, she now has speech

My name she calls, scissors in her reach

By the time I see her move it is already too late

Now you all know the tale of my terrible fate

Gruesome Gals

A is for Alma who killed him with an ax
B is for Bernice who filled him with bullets
C is for Caroline who diced him with a cleaver
D is for Dawn who blew him up with dynamite
E is for Emily who shocked him with electricity
F is for Fanny who caught him on fire
G is for Georgia who shot him with a gun
H is for Helen who beat him with a hammer
I is for Idella who murdered him with a ice-pick
J is for Jewel who split his head with a jack-hammer
K is for Kimi who stabbed him with a knife
L is for Libby who hid him where they will never look
M is for Mary who changed his medicine
N is for Nicole who stabbed him with needles
O is for Opal who gave him plenty of opium
P is for Penny who drowned him in a pool
Q is for Quintana who poisoned his quiche
R is for Rhonda who broke all his ribs
S is for Sarah who whacked him with a shovel
T is for Treva who ran over him with a truck
U is for Uva who did things to him that were too ugly
V is for Velma who fed him snake venom
W is for Wilma who beat him with a whip
X is for Xana who gave him a bottle marked X
Y is for Yvonne who strangled him with yarn
Z is for Zia who feed him to the zebras

Step-Mother

Today Step-mother is in charge, but I'll win the game

This phony mother's time is at her end, she is to blame

She is evil, vicious and mean; I want to settle the score

I'll trip her down the stairs she'll be bleeding and sore

When she takes her bubble bath, she'll meet my pet leeches

Choking hazards are high; when I feed her pits from cherries and peaches

She'll soon find out that two spoonfuls of rat poison are in her tea

I'll tie her to a boat, for a Viking funeral, and then she'll be off to be lost at sea

We will play house and she is the ugly old lamp, I'll put her finger in a socket

She will soon be a star above; I've just tied her to a rocket

Ten Little girls

Ten little girls lay dead in a perfect row

Ten little girls had nowhere hide, nowhere to go

Ten little girls were bloody from head to toe

Ten little girls were all naughty, don't you know

Ten little girls all shared the same little foe

Ten little girls should have been nice to Jessie Jo

The Zoo

Our class took a trip to the zoo

I let out the rhinos, what harm will they do?

I let out the bears and the lions too

A Bunch of Nuts

A man came to in a strange room, and realized that he was restrained.

"Help!" he shouted, trying to get free from the chair that he was tied to.

A little boy, age ten, and a little girl, age eight, walked in, "Hello", they said.

"Help me!" he cried out, still trying to escape.

The boy spoke, "I heard you are allergic to peanuts!"

"Yes, why do you care?" his voice was full of anger.

"Lillie, do you have the nuts?" The boy asked.

"Yes, Edmond, I do!" the girl giggled as she showed off the ten-pound bag.

"Why are you doing this to me, you evil little brats?" he yelled.

Edmond smiled, "We wanted to see how many you could eat before you die!"

Lillie opened the bag, "Are you ready, mister?" she asked with a laugh.

"Alright," the man yelled once more, "Tell me why!"

Lillie spoke, "Our Mother told us to make our own fun!", as she put a peanut into his mouth.

One by one they fed the man peanuts, until the bag was empty, and when he died they weren't too sure.

"I lost count!" cried out Lillie.

"Me, too!" shouted Edmond.

Lillie smiled, "Let's get another one!"

Farewell

Farewell, farewell, she fell down the hill

Farewell, farewell, he took one too many pill

Farewell, farewell, she liked to play with fire

Farewell, farewell, he was choked by a wire

Farewell, farewell, she put her finger in the socket

Farewell, farewell, he was tied to a rocket

Farewell, farewell, she was eaten by a dog

Farewell, farewell, he was smashed by a log

Farewell, farewell, she was shot

Farewell, farewell, he got what he got

Farewell, farewell, she was drowned

Farewell, farewell, his body was never found

Princess

Up in the high stone tower, reaching, reaching for the sky
clear and blue

A lovely young princess in a long pink gown blows
thousands of kisses to you

The yellow sun is shining; this is love, true love a feeling
that is new!

Scaling the ivy green covered tower, careful not to lose a
glove or shoe

Halfway up passing purple flowers, you realize for her this
is easy to do

In the tower you see bones on the floor and blood red, a
deep glimmering hue

The princess eats you and says with a hiccup, "He was
tastier than the last two"

Sister

My big sister she was always real mean

So I made a friend with big teeth and eyes green

He would live under her bed

I promised he would be well fed

One night she was very bad

I warned her not to make me mad

She broke the head right off my pretty doll

My monster friend's name I then did call

Its large furry hand grabbed her by her face

And pulled her under the bed not leaving a trace

The Waiting

In the morning as you brush your teeth I am waiting in the shower

You hear me breathing and you start to shake and cower

I hide in the dark corner of your closet and wait

Using your favorite soft sweater as bait

The garage is my playground, this you don't like

You have to pass me by when you get your little red bike

When you come home from school I am under the kitchen sink

You try to tell your parents and they don't know what to think

As you try to sleep I am lying beneath your bed

My breath is the cool breeze you feel upon your head

Your parents didn't believe you when you said I was there

Now they won't be able to find you anywhere

Day and Night

Day and night
Day and night
I feel their eyes on me

Filling me with fright
I feel their eyes on me
Where they are I cannot see
Watching and waiting
They are there

They are there
They are there
All the time
Everywhere and nowhere

Everywhere and nowhere
Always in my mind
Filling me with darkness
Filling me with fear

Darkness and fear
Darkness and fear
Taking all peace
They are always near

Silly Lily

There once was a girl named Lily

Who did something very silly

She took my favorite toy from me

I asked for it back immediately

She answered with a sneer

And I warned her to beware

She laughed at me

Then tried to flee

As I took out my knife

And took away her life

I smile and I beam

As I still hear her scream

There once was a girl named Lily

Who did something very silly

Just Desserts

Do not eat the cookies that Mariah makes
She's always sure to use poison when she bakes
Also stay away from her pies and her cakes

Bedtime

Mother told me that it would be alright

That there was nothing hiding in the night

Nothing under the bed with sharp teeth that bite

She tucked me in and told me goodnight

Said "Sweet dreams" and turned off the light

She didn't see the red eyes glowing bright

Hungry Holly

Hi, my name is Hungry Holly. I'm the gift all the little
girls want. I'm the prettiest doll you've ever seen; I have
long golden curls and big blue eyes. I come with three
dresses, an apron and a little kitchen set. When you hold
my hand I say, "I'm hungry Holly, feed me!" And you
better, or else!

Last Christmas I was a gift for Olivia Gross. She was seven
and wanted me for the past six months. When she
unwrapped me she let out a yell, "I Love her!" She held
my hand all day long and I kept asking for her to feed me,
but then she started to play with her other toys! She left
me all alone. I was starving! Hours and hours passed, I
was still not fed. Then Olivia's mother told her and her
two brothers to go to bed. Olivia came over to me. "At
last," I thought. She held my hand once more, "I'm
Hungry Holly, feed me." I said for the hundredth time!
The little brat just kissed me, "Good night, Holly."
She put me back in my box! I was starving and I needed
food. I was going to make sure that she never treated
another doll like this again!
I waited until Olivia was asleep then I quietly crept out of
the box, being sure not to let the lid slam. By morning I
had returned to my box and Olivia had not moved. Soon
she awoke and came back over to me, smiling as if she had
not done anything wrong. She held my hand and again I
spoke, this time saying, "I told you I was hungry."
"Mommy, Holly says something else! Holly says
something else!" The obnoxious girl exclaimed. But her
Mommy never came. Neither did her Daddy or her two
stupid brothers. She ran to her parents' bedroom, only to

find that their bedding was shredded to pieces and everything was soaked in blood. The stupid little girl started to cry. She stopped when she felt something touch her leg. She touched my hand once more, like a little idiot. I said, "I'm still a little peckish."
All I can say is the Gross family was quite delicious.

Sandlin

Haunting

Haikus

A Chill in the Air: A Collection of Stories and Poetry

Sandlin

I once had a fright
Spine tingles as fear remains
My goosebumps linger

She answered the door
The pillow silenced her scream
I left the remains

In a shallow grave
I covered the body with dirt
I still hear the cries

The telephone rings
A voice unknown to me speaks
"You have until noon"

I ran to the hall
I thought I heard a scream
There I found the body

Bubbling cauldron
A laughing witch is stirring
The potion is done

My blood is flowing
These veins are nearly bled out
There is nothing left

I hear the footsteps
They're haunting my dreams at night
They're getting louder

Just four little drops
And then he will be no more
Mother taught me well

Way deep in the woods
In cottage I await
Visit if you will

I never liked him
He was always in the way
Now I can have peace

Down in your basement
A beast is waiting for you
And I'm so hungry

Sandlin

Darkness overcomes
Hope vanishes with the light
Now I am alone

Trembling I wait here
Knowing that I cannot run
My time has come now

Run or hide in vain
It is coming for you
There is no escape

Terrifying cries
Welcome to your nightmare
You cannot leave now

Watching you at night
Yellow eyes glow in the dark
It is feeding time

The temperature drops
A shadow comes towards you
There is no hope

Growls fill the still air
You are motionless with fear
They're back and hungry

She was on the floor
The bottle was in her hand
Poison on her breath

Deep inside your mind
They all tell you what to do
Willingly you act

Dark forms are outside
Watching and waiting for you
You belong with them

Sandlin

Helpless you struggle
Fighting against the current
Waves wash over you

Look in the mirror
The reflection is not yours
You have set it free

You cannot forget
Desperate cries fill your ears
They will never stop

Do not try to fight
There is no hope of escape
Accept your new fate

All the lights burn out
I hear soft footsteps coming
It's too late to run

Fresh baked cookies
Wrapped nicely with a bow
Eat them if you dare

Olive pits are in the pie
They become stuck in your throat
Your face is turning blue

Blood painted faces
Are peeking through the green forest
There's nowhere to go

She sits on the crescent moon
Waiting for someone to sleep
She brings you nightmares

Skeletons dance
Hypnotizing me into their grave
I'm now part of the earth

In this awful place
Dark things occur, bad strange things
Now be quiet, he is coming

Sandlin

Their voices echo
All of them were bad people
That's why I did it

She was hidden away
In hopes to keep us safe
She has been released

I watch you closely
Waiting for you to come here
Then I'll pull you in

Deep into the water
Among the wreaked pirate ships
That is where the body is

Yes, the stone reads my name
But I am still in this house
You are the intruder

I'm the rapping on the glass
The noise that is up in the attic
I am your shadow

The doll's head just moved
Her eyes are fixed on me
Evil spirit inside

A haunting whistle
Echoes across the cold, empty room
I know the ghost very well

Buried in the ground
A crime done seeking vengeance
No one hears the cries

Stars fall from the sky
Screaming fills the midnight air
The end is coming

Sandlin

She is always there
Waiting, waiting for her chance
At last you are hers

Flames burn bright and high
Destruction looms all around
She warned you about this

The End

It is a dark and rainy day

Until the storm passes, in my home I will stay

Not once do I hear the morning birds sing

So quiet, not a noise heard, not even a telephone ring

I turn around to see that my treasured collections have gone amiss

Not much seems to remain in this timeless vast abyss

My stomach is not empty, nor is it full

I have no hunger, in this place there is no rule

My cedar chest gives off no scent

I must tell my story, I need to vent

I step out of my door and walk the dusty road where headstones stand

I reach out to one and touch my name with my own hand

Acknowledgements

We would like to thank some of the many people who made it possible for this book to exist

Our family and friends – thank you for always supporting, loving and encouraging us

The Elwood Library Writing Group – thank you for giving us a place for our creativity to grow

Aragorn – thank you for all of your help and advice

Emily Smith and the brothers Hight – thank you for bringing our vision to life

Sarah E. - The kind re-teller of fairy tales

The late Georgia A. Ellis- thank you for being one of Elwood's greatest poets

The late Mildred S. Hunter – thank you for the poems left behind

All illustrations provided by free websites